RULES FOR OLD MEN WAITING

Born in Tsingtao, China, of British parents, and educated at Oxford, Peter Pouncey is a classicist who left for the United States at the end of the sixties to do a PhD at Columbia University, and stayed on there. He was for many years a Professor of Classics and is now President Emeritus of Amherst College. He is married and lives in New York.

PETER POUNCEY

Rules for Old Men Waiting

VINTAGE BOOKS
London

Published by Vintage 2006

2 4 6 8 10 9 7 5 3 1

Copyright © Peter Pouncey 2005

Peter Pouncey has asserted his right under the Copyright,
Designs and Patents Act, 1988 to be identified as the author
of this work

First published in the United States of America in 2005 by
Random House

First published in Great Britain in 2005 by
Chatto & Windus

Vintage
Random House, 20 Vauxhall Bridge Road, London SW1V 2SA

Random House Australia (Pty) Limited
20 Alfred Street, Milsons Point, Sydney,
New South Wales 2061, Australia

Random House New Zealand Limited
18 Poland Road, Glenfield, Auckland 10, New Zealand

Random House (Pty) Limited
Isle of Houghton, Corner of Boundary Road & Carse O'Gowrie,
Houghton, 2198, South Africa

The Random House Group Limited Reg. No. 954009
www.randomhouse.co.uk/vintage

A CIP catalogue record for this book
is available from the British Library

ISBN 9780099483571 (from Jan 2007)
ISBN 0099483572

Printed and bound in Great Britain by
Cox & Wyman Limited, Reading, Berkshire

FOR KATHERINE

she brought him well
to his remembrance

And it shall come to pass afterward, that
I shall pour out my spirit upon all flesh. . . .
Your old men shall dream dreams,
your young men shall see visions.

Joel 2:28

Contents

Rules for Old Men Waiting

CHAPTER 1

Rules to Stop the Rot

The house and the old man were well matched, both large framed and failing fast. The house had a better excuse, MacIver thought; he was eighty, but the house was older than the Republic, had been a century old when Thoreau walked the Cape, though he couldn't have seen it tucked away in the nondescript maze of scrub oak. It had been the willful seclusion of the place that had appealed to them when they first saw it—that and the equally hidden pool, about two minutes away through their woods, which must have decided the builder to choose the site. The oaks grew more substantial as they approached the pond, but the casual visitor would not have registered their rising height as the ground fell away down to the water. But when the path did its last little jink through the thicket of spare mossy trunks and last year's leaves, you stood on the edge of something suddenly spacious. A stretch of almost two hundred yards of water, more than fifty wide, a *glade* of water, fringed at both ends by sedge and reeds, shaded along the sides by the larger oaks. Bird-loud by day, redwings and warblers in and out of the reeds and busy water-traffic of ducks, and even, for a few seasons, the stately progressions of a pair of swans; owls with their fluttery hoots at night, and very often at the far end beyond a fallen log, the hunched figure of a black-crowned night heron, the grim presiding judge executing sentence on a surprising number of small fish and frogs.

Margaret and he had watched the pond over the years at every hour in every season. In summer, it was their swimming pool, where they swam naked at any time of day. Often on hot August nights, they would have a last dip before bed. They would take one towel between them, and no flashlight, because the night sky overhead was bright enough to light their way down the faint, twisting path. MacIver, an energetic but clumsy swimmer, would thrash the water into turbulence out into the deep and then make for shore, and try to use the towel as little as possible, to leave it dry for Margaret. She would go on a while longer, parting the water gently in her rhythmic breast-stroke, the moonlight playing on her wet hair with each forward surge, a sleek and quiet otter. He would lose her in the shadowed background at the far end, and peer with great concentration into the dark, to catch the first ripple of her return. When she finally waded towards the bank where he was standing, he would stay motionless trying to register the first moment when he could see into her silhouette, and detect the dark roundness of her nipples and the triangle of her pubic hair. Then she would let him dry her off, and they would go home to bed.

In other seasons, dressed for the weather, they would take their station under one of the oaks, his back to the trunk, with Margaret sitting between his legs, and simply let the life of the pool evolve around them. They had seen families of deer come down to drink, they had seen a raccoon balance on a log and try to fish with his paw, and one evening in the last of the light, they had seen a great horned owl sail out from the tree above them and swoop on a small rabbit on the other side of the pond. They had heard the short squeal, and seen the inert furry bundle dangling from the bird's talons as he passed over them on his return. Many foxes, and once he would have sworn a bobcat, though it can't have been, padding along the far bank and back into the trees. You never knew what you would see. MacIver named the pond the Blind Pool, from a favorite boyhood story, though it was called Frog Pond on his geodetic map, and Margaret had called the house Night Heron House in honor of the constant sentinel standing by his fallen branch; she did a fine woodcut of him, too, which still hung inside the front door.

It was a traditional Cape house, but on a larger scale than was usual, a bold architect's airy enlargement. The front rooms were high ceilinged and framed with more massive beams, and instead of the usual chicken-run stairs inside the front door, there was a handsome Y-shaped staircase down a wide hall, breaking at a little landing halfway up and then splitting to left and right for the upper rooms. A Victorian owner had widened the two front windows and bowed them, letting in more light, and then had built a porch between the two bows, with central steps up to the front door and a simple railing on either side. The house stood by itself in a clearing, which you had to maintain vigilantly: half a summer, and the locust, oak, and birch sprigs would be crowding onto the grass. Original glass in many panes; the shapes of things outside alternately clouded and cleared as your eyes moved across the windows. Original two-foot-wide floorboards and paneling on the walls, flouting an ancient Massachusetts statute reserving such width for the absent king. A cool, self-possessed house of mellow resonance, as if you were living inside a spacious cello. Nothing too decorative.

They had three and a half decades to set their rhythms, com-

ing and going to their secret fastness, the Night Heron House
with its woods and pond. When Margaret fell ill and the doctors
said they could do no more for her, they had moved to the Cape,
as they had always planned in such a case, "year-round"; in fact,
she had three seasons left, fall to spring, 1986–1987. At first the
house had seemed to banish sickness. They had moved their bed
into the living room, so she would not have to manage the stairs,
but in the large, airy space she bustled light-footed as ever; she
set up her easel, and started a series of tree-scapes framed by the
windows at different times of the day. The trees on the canvas
got barer, MacIver noticed, as the season turned, but the paintings got lighter, at first because the angle of focus was raised to
allow more cloud and sky, and at the end, in the unfinished ones,
because the marks on the prepared white canvas, while precisely
made, were fainter, less assertive: the effect left on her only
viewer was of being pulled in her art past the blank of whiteness
to the vanishing point of thin air.

As winter approached, they would still visit the pond on
good days, though they didn't stay long to absorb its more
furtive movement; they would come out at the end of the path
and stand a few moments looking, an old couple supporting
each other in a lover's stance, heads inclined towards each other,
his rangy arm around her frail shoulders, her mittened hand
around his waist. Then they would work their way back; she only
needed a sighting, it seemed. Things were moving faster for
them now, forcing changes they could not plan. In no time the
number of hours she could be up each day, the number of feet
she could walk, were shortening on them. By the end of February, she was confined to bed, daily falling further away from him
deeper into sickness. He was ill himself, he knew, but nothing to
this. First weekly, then twice a week, he would make grim sallies

to the drugstore for the morphine prescribed from New York, and come back as fast as he dared, fearful of finding another visible weakening. There was no talk of going somewhere else for final care. It would end here, in this room. He would read to her, coax her to eat a little, play Mozart to her, spin new tales she would like about his boyhood on Loch Affric, and games and battles farther afield. When she drowsed, he would stay sitting on in the bentwood rocker through the fading afternoon. She would wake up and read his unguarded face; she could see her fierce old Scot being gentled out of character by his own secret illness, never to be mentioned, and by grief.

It was all grotesquely new to him; he was not a man who had ever willingly let things be taken out of his hands. Sometimes she would send him on small missions, to shake him out of his spellbound broodings. She would ask him to go down to the pond, "and report back on your findings." At first in the winter, he would have to work hard for interesting gleanings to take back to her—animal tracks on the frozen pond, an air bubble caught in the creamy ice inshore around the heron's branch, the number of trees deep he could count in the leafless screen of woods across the pond, viewed from the oak where they hung the towel. When the grudging days of early spring arrived, and the trees were fretted more with undergrowth, the views foreshortened, but there was more to report. One day in late April, he had taken her back a box turtle, patterned in a smart brown and yellow plaid, but built a little too high off the ground, like the old Volkswagen Beetle, to be aerodynamically sound. MacIver had put him on the quilt, and the little fellow had finally stuck his head out of his shell and taken a couple of steps, before pooping quite impressively right there on the bed. Margaret had given him the Scottish name of Archibald, and insisted that

MacIver take him back to exactly the same leaves in which he had found him, with the added gift of a lettuce leaf for his pains. She died three days after that, on the first soft day that promised full-blooded spring.

As Margaret had feared would be the case, MacIver did not do well after she had gone. He let himself go, and he let the house go. He knew it was happening and he felt badly about it as far as the house was concerned, but he didn't seem able to do much about it, except fitfully. His concentration was gone, along with the object of his attention. There was a backlog of work due on the house; they had loved it and cared for it year after year, as it needed and deserved, but in the fall MacIver had persuaded Margaret against all previous habits to delay some of the chores to the spring; they should hunker down and enjoy each other quietly, without ladders looming and workers banging. She had been sick enough to agree, but the house was showing its frailty now quite markedly; it was no longer a matter of cleaning gutters, checking storm windows, and calling the exterminator to keep the termites at bay. The fabric of the house was sagging visibly on the eastern side, and he was sure it needed a new roof. And what else? He mentally checked off the items he knew about—siding on the windward face of the house, boiler, always feeble, cheating him of more and more degrees against the thermostat (unless it was the cold, or the windows?), two sagging, buckled gutters. In the end, he did not call the contractors, because he did not want them to open up the house and tell him how bad it was. And he did not call them because he still did not want their banging, their company, or even their secret sympathy. Bereavement seemed to work on him as a kind of blanket allergy, making him edgy and irritable to all the outside world.

And of course it was reciprocal: the world receded on him.

Even his own Blind Pool seemed to shun him as an interloper. The lens of the water, which had taken in a full orbit of creatures and their activities, their presence and their shadows, and held them for key moments for the two of them to share and admire, now stared blankly upwards, blind indeed. He could tell that his ability to focus, to fix on a detail and hold it, had deserted him, and the loss of it had weakened his grasp on the place. He did not really seem able to see what was happening anymore.

Once he made an effort to put this right by willpower alone: he would make himself a botanist along the lines of Margaret herself, who could identify every wildflower she encountered, including the tiny creepers you were about to step on, barely showing more than two petals above the clutter of leaves around them. She had assembled a beautiful library of Victorian botanical books, gorgeously illustrated with her own kind of painterly eye. With these in hand, he would beat himself into an amateur botanist. He went for walks and collected samples of wildflowers and grasses he did not know; he intended to study such things as root systems, the deepening shades of color at the base of petals, the precise veining and edge of every blade of grass. "Focus!" he enjoined himself. He sat at the dining room table with the fine old Victorian guides, his glasses on the end of his nose and his samples lined up in front of him, and announced to the empty room, "We will now name names." Then he picked up an unoffending but anonymous plant, with small white flowers and long skinny leaves, and asked like an inquisitor: "What is your bloody name?" He riffled through the books, occasionally coming up with a winner: "Your name," he declared in patiently didactic tones, "is Seneca Snakeroot," and made a note of it on the pad beside him. He held himself to the work as long as he could, matching specimens to the elegant paintings in the guides, and putting doubtful ones aside for reexamination when he drew a blank, but the whole exercise was painful and pointless: he wasn't meant to be a taxonomist—his interest in the work had no root. Why labor to put names on things, when there was no one there to say them to? He persevered for a few days with diminishing returns, and then the line of samples was left to wilt on the table, exuding a hot acidic scent, like weeds cut and left lying after the scythe. When they had fully dried and started to break up, he picked up the paper they were on and slid them unceremoniously into the trash.

Without taxonomy, the summer went on, and he could not really have said whether it was wet or dry, hot or cold. He went swimming a couple of times, and after the second attempt emerged shivering. His own illness was now hard for him to ignore. Passing the full-length mirror in the wardrobe door on his way to the shower, he surveyed with detachment the skeleton he would soon be, seeing through the paper-thin, blue-traced skin stretched over knobs: it was true, the bodies of old men were unseemly. Spidery on the outside, it seemed the whole web of connection was also fraying within; all his old orthopedic injuries were playing themselves out again, right knee dislocating itself, right shoulder clamped in arthritis so he could not raise his arm chest-high. His walk had slowed to a shuffle, testing each footfall.

Still, there were better days, when the cloud cover broke, the step seemed resolute and the mind clear. One day after Labor Day and a big September storm, he felt well enough to survey his pond once more, and was rewarded with a startling sign: he had barely made his way down the path to full view of the water, when an osprey, straying God knows how far afield, appeared, a stark apparition with the fierce black markings on the white frame, an obvious intruder making no effort to camouflage himself. The big hawk cruised one length of the pool nonchalantly first, circled round to the right, started another run a little more purposefully, saw what he was looking for, and made his strike. The descent was remarkably steep, the whole body taut, wings raised back and feet extended like locked landing gear, then the water pierced and the talons clenched on quite a large fish, while the huge wingspan worked to restore forward motion, feet and fish now trailing behind, scattering drops of water on the shattered green glass. MacIver watched frozen with excitement at the athleticism of the catch. "You like predators, don't you?" Margaret had said years before at his exultation over the owl. "I love big obvious birds with style," he had said, "but I love their victims, too." So here was another one, another sign to him, writ large, he thought, to hit home to his too blatant nature. From owl to osprey, rabbit to fish. It seemed to put a seal on all the pool had offered them both over the thirty-five years. He was not confident he could visit it again. But what he had loved it for, he now saw, was not these extravagant gestures but its reserve, showing its secrets, big or small, in its own time, never profligate, keeping him humble, never an initiate, always a patient believer waiting for the next revelation. It was the closest he came to observing one of Margaret's insightful cautions: "Don't go so much for the staginess. Go for the deeper, quieter rhythms, and you'll get some peace out of them!" Now he was grateful to the pool for making itself so vivid to him again, but he could leave it to its measured life apart; he would know it was playing out its habitual patterns those few steps through the woods away from him and his beleaguered house.

Without his noticing it, the fall had come and gone. How the year came crashing down again to winter! He had not fixed anything in the house, he had made no contact with former colleagues or friends, and he was not eating, but wasting away. It was as though he was rehearsing once more the slow attrition that he had watched in Margaret, following the steps of her emaciation to a quick end. But that was not way he saw it. The reason he could do none of the necessary things to take care of himself, on the few occasions when he thought of them, was that he was preoccupied elsewhere. Great gusts of emotion, of weeping but also of rage and strange exultation, and powerful images, full of color and detail, seemed to have taken hold of him.

Day after day, there was a regular progression of symptoms leading to an upspringing of visions and fantasy. He would increasingly find himself listless and tired, often after he had been up less than an hour. Whether he had been reading a book or doing some chore in the kitchen, he would become aware he was not thinking clearly—and the cause of this he saw as physical. An actual cloud, he felt, was stealing across his brain, evening mist across marshy ground. Banging himself on the side of his head with his open palm did not clear it. His listlessness seemed to push his hands and feet out to a great distance from his control. At this point he would become afraid that if he remained standing up, he might become dizzy and fall, and he would move slowly back to his bed and lie down. Sinking back into the bedclothes was at first a relief, and there was often a pleasant sense of rocking or swaying there, as though he had returned from a dinner with too much wine in him, or was lying in a hammock out of doors. Then the pictures would start up in his head, taking him over.

There were various strands of images supplied to him, mostly separate but occasionally running into each other. More than once a weird double feature played through his mind. The two parts were certainly different in tone, the first a somber art movie of Margaret, almost silent, filmed in a series of gloomy interiors. Heavy curtains around leaded windows and a pewter sky beyond. It was not their house, but it was Margaret all right. He had to peer to see her, to bring her near, but when he managed to focus, he saw her always distracted or agitated. He could hear his own voice talking to her, quite loudly, probably insisting too much, but she wasn't paying attention anyway. Studying her expression closely, he saw flickers of distaste and irritation around her mouth. "I can tell you often did not like me," he said. "Only towards the end," she said finally and flatly, and looking away from him: "I didn't like the way things were going."

There were several things that troubled him about these sequences, one of which was that they left some hurt behind when he came to himself; another was his puzzlement about the mockery of his own inner mind, offering her back to him as unloving, unconnected, half-lit and inanimate, against all the patterns of his conscious memory and longings. He was not well equipped to pursue this line of thought, but the effect these pictures had was to screw him more tightly into his loneliness.

Then abruptly the pictures changed. With his feeble, wandering brain it was hard to keep track of time, but often they seemed to change in the same session, day or night. Wan scenes of recrimination would give way to war footage. This could not have been more different. The colors here were the bright orange, crimson, and black of exploding shells. Men in battle fatigues with small arms were running athletically and confidently among them, making their cut at the right point to avoid the next flash, like good broken-field runners. There was a tone of arrogance over the whole scene; some commander's voice could be heard in the background making a radio report, clear above the static: "We've got the brains and the muscle, and we're blowing them away." MacIver had to admit he liked watching this scene; he did not know what cause the men were fighting for, but he liked the fact that they were invulnerable, disappearing at a steady clip into the middle distance. You could tell they would soon stifle the artillery fire bursting among them; they would cut it off at the source. MacIver had been in the navy himself: where did all these soldiers come from?

He would come to himself from these dreaming sequences, weaker still. And colder. Outside there was now a winter worth attending to. Large hanging icicles from the overflowing gutters above grew downward across the living room and bedroom windows, and glinted sharply in the afternoon light; but however brightly the sun blazed, day after day it had no warmth—as far as he could see, not one pendant drop of water ever formed, dangled, or fell from the icy points. When he looked past them into the glare of white on white, the trees seemed to have receded, grey striations whittled away by the snow plastered on their windward side; and the shadows they cast on the snowbanks as the sun fell were weaker too, no darker than a sickly blue.

The cold reached indoors with a vengeance. Among his many omissions was his failure to lay in firewood over the summer for the Vermont Castings stove, to supplement the pathetic furnace in the basement in just such a season as this. The house had been toasty warm the previous winter, when the stove had been kept at full blast trying to send its glow of comfort to Margaret's shivering bones under the layers of blankets. The whole woodpile across the lawn had been consumed in this effort. Now his failure to replenish it loomed larger every day. He still had hot water for his shower, because that had an electric heater;

but it was only a matter of time, he thought, before the ever-intrusive cold wrapped itself around some standing pipe and eventually burst it. Surprising it hadn't happened before. He could drag his finger through the crusty ice on the inside of windowpanes in any room now. Lying in bed at night, often in his navy greatcoat, he could hear the old house groaning around him, shrinking in on itself under the onslaught. They were both just lying there waiting. Both of them old and cold. Margaret gone. Everything inside and everything outside frozen in its aches and pains to a tight immobility. One bold move and something would snap.

And finally did. He had been making one more effort: to go out and glean something that would burn from around the exhausted woodpile or the edge of the woods. Slow and steady, no athletic moves. Except it was slow and jerky, at every step hating his own brittleness, his feeble shuffle-lurch, small, short mouse-breaths.

He had not got far, but he had got out the door. And then the frozen porch collapsed under him. He was pausing, planning the next step, and the porch, hitherto seemingly integral with the house, had skewed sideways and bowed; slightly wobbly undulations gave way slowly to a more systematic curve, a glazed path of least resistance, which he had slid down without injury. "Let the angels lead you down"—and indeed they had let him down lightly.

But quality will out. Sap and purposes run on, even after anyone has given up intending them. The old four-square porch had given up on its rotting steps, and designed itself instead this ramp—its simple railing for a moment damn near a balustrade. The odd steel pin must have stayed tensile, and permitted a twist instead of a shatter. The effect was not ungraceful, if the eye hadn't been taught to expect something straight. The slow-motion image fixed itself in his mind, but there was commotion inside him. Shock and shame for the house giving way, and yes, for his own collapse. He lay on the new ramp counting his bones, and a sad resolution formed in his mind: *I must retrench.*

He clambered slowly back inside the house, and allowed himself to rest after the nasty shock of his fall. Head a little bowed, poor old man's nape meekly exposed, hands limp in his lap, he sat and let the agitation ebb away. A small decent voice inside him whispered, *You need help.* But it was never as clear or insistent as the voice that kept saying, *I must retrench.* He still had room to retreat through, safe inside his house. It would be, he thought, a planned withdrawal as needed, to his last redoubt, his bed. They would have to come and get him.

Breathing a little more regularly now, and playing back in his mind the sudden slide, a piece of self-knowledge struck him: he had been trying to finish himself off. The porch had preempted it—cut him benignly short. But he could see how it had been meant to end. Not even wrapped against elements, wearing simply his old Marks & Spencer blue cardigan, he had shuffled out into the knife-edged cold, like Captain Oates leaving the tent. He must have understood that he could not crunch his way out and back; the snow had drifted and crusted with ice. He was barely strung together orthopedically, and it was nowadays even money whether he could putter safely across a level floor. Outside, one sudden lurch through the treacherous crust and he would have been down for good.

He could see the fall now. A little floundering but not for long. Everywhere he grasped for purchase crumbling away, pointless to struggle: the hurtful cold had already fastened on him, and was eating into him. The snow would compose itself again into a groove molded to the shape of his body. He could see himself lying there, one leg of his corduroys pulled up, showing the long johns, one arm stretched out ahead, the hand holding perhaps two or three pathetic twigs—the extent of his foraging. A small patch of pure ice around his mouth and nose, where feeble breathing had melted the snow briefly. In that cold, half an hour would have finished him, sculpting a frozen tableau for the local newspapers a few months ahead: HISTORIAN'S BODY FOUND BY SUMMER PEOPLE.

He pondered the picture for a while, and concluded that he did not like it. That was not the way he wanted to go. His mood was changing, the old adrenaline tank filling up again with bile and ebullience. He had been challenging himself where he was bound to lose. He should play it wily. Redefine the rules of the game so he was bound to win. Keep the mind engaged, and have fun doing it, not drifting and not hounding himself.

Some decisions started to shape themselves. Let me be to my sad self hereafter kind. He would set himself no more humiliating physical challenges, and he would no longer waste time trying to figure where he went wrong. (Where he went wrong at this point was in living on after Margaret died.) He should devise a plan, to harbor resources best for a kind of holding action. He should do things every day to keep himself alert and as happy as possible. If you are going to go under, it shouldn't be from the weight of self-pity alone. He must make rules to hold himself together, like Descartes holing up by his winter stove to question the very foundation of things—exactly the kind of task he no longer needed to set himself! But let's have rules, by all means.

Over the next two days, pottering around the house, he evolved his Rules for Winter Watch / Rules for the Inside

Game: what they really were was a plan to take back his life, until he could give it away on an acceptable basis. Meanwhile, it would be healthy for him to tell himself what to do.

1. Keep personally clean.
2. Make bed every morning, and clean house twice a week.
3. Dress warmly, and light fire when necessary, burning least important things first.
4. Eat regularly.
5. Play music and read.
6. Television only in the evening, except for weekend and seasonal showdown sports.
7. Work every morning. Nap in afternoon if needed.

He wrote these down and read them over. They offered, he thought, a simple skeleton of the well-ordered life for a feeble old man. He found nothing to take exception to. But over the next two days, as he continued to wander still a little uncertainly through the house, he came to realize that some of the rules needed further clarification if he was to act on them. Rules Three, Four, and Seven in particular needed glossing, regulations for the application of the law. He took a fresh piece of paper, headed it Rules for Winter Watch: *Reformed State,* and added further subsets, under the headings Correct Order for Burning Household Objects, Calculations for Rationing Food Per Diem, and Appropriate Work for Winter Watch.

On Rule Three, he remembered a passage of Newman, doddered over to the shelf, found it in the book, and wrote it down: "Hear Newman on Saint John, 'The ventures of faith': 'He had to bear a length of years in loneliness, exile, and weakness. He had to experience the dreariness of being solitary, when those whom he loved had been summoned away. He had to live in his own thoughts, without familiar friend. He was as a man moving his goods into a far country, who at intervals and by portions sends them before him, till his present abode is well nigh unfurnished.'" That's the spirit, MacIver thought. Let it all go, one foot in the grave and one bag packed. We shall go to our end in the warm glow of the past, burning up the memories, all the clutter given back. What are the rules for dismantling / consuming the things of the past?

a) Retain the beautiful and useful.
b) Of wooden things, no articles of fine craftsmanship will be burnt. Consume journeyman chairs etc.
c) Margaret's pictures to be kept. Otherwise, picture frames before pictures.
d) Books of rival scholars and other trash, before good books and my own.

MacIver was pleased with his subset of rules for burning. But on old Rule Four, he felt he needed more guidance; and he certainly needed improvement on his recent performance. The fact that he had not been eating regularly must account, at least in part, for his sharp decline over the last few months. Perhaps it also explained the images that assaulted him: had malnutrition made him visionary? He was inclined to think not. But the fact was he no longer knew what food he had left. Calculating back over the last hazy months, he thought it must have been a day or so after he saw the osprey, with his euphoria still in place, that he had made his last expedition for food. Ah, yes, he remembered, after Labor Day, when the shops and beaches had cleared, and the lines were short at the checkout counter. Why not, he had thought, pile a lot of stuff into the car, and save himself from doing it on some crowded holiday?

He had thrown himself into filling up two carts, muttering to himself as he trundled the aisles, the Flying Scotsman victualing his phantom ship. There was method in his madness. He laid his base with businesslike rods of pasta in their flat packets, good for storage, and hefty cans of Italian tomatoes pendant in their juice, depicted by some Florentine fresco painter on fine archaic labels; then bags of potatoes, yams, rice, flour. Sugar, butter, olive oil, tea and coffee, cans of soup, bacon. The freezer was working as far as he knew, so he laid in stores of frozen orange juice and vegetables. No scurvy on this ship, even if under Margaret's sway all such things had to be fresh. She had once come upon him launching a slug of half-melted concentrate from the pulpy container of juice into a jug. Her horror had been quite unfeigned.

As the carts filled, his spirits rose, and with them his self-indulgence. The top layer of the second cart presented the further reaches of his taste: Tiptree's Tawny Marmalade, two bottles of single malt whisky, six of Meursault, half a drum of Stilton, dark amber maple syrup, a jar of stem ginger, a small tin of foie gras. He might, he thought, dip into such things on rare banner days—after rounding the Horn, perhaps. The girl at the checkout counter was surprised at the quantity. "You're certainly laying in supplies, Mr. MacIver: you expecting a flood or something?"

"That, and a long voyage to an unknown port," he had said. She had yelled *Bon voyage!* to him as he had trundled the second loaded cart out to the car.

As he lifted the big grocery bags out of the back seat and lugged them into the house, his euphoria had left him abruptly. The house smelled lonely and unkept—what would he do with all this food? He would prepare it messily and munch at it alone. Into the emptiness loomed suddenly with intense longing a sensuous image of Margaret, in the endless halcyon days when they had first come to the Cape to play some thirty-five years before—Margaret gliding barefoot around the kitchen and cheerfully stashing food. How she had loved doing it! Cabinet doors flicked open and shut, each inviting a wonderfully particular set of foodstuffs, all destined in her mind for a series of dinner recipes planned for the days ahead. But this was no monthly or even weekly ritual. Daily the prospective delights had to be renewed and extended, the bags of plenty distributed into the little wooden cupboards. There were herbs and exotic vegetables and fruits out of season, there was rich foreign chocolate for bedtime. "This is like an ad for the happy singing peasants in Italy," he remarked, leaning against the sink nursing his beer, and enjoying the cheerful bustle without helping. "Ecco, monsignore," she sang in her pretty light soprano, holding two Bosc pears up against her breasts and spinning, so that her flared skirt rose and showed her girlish legs and panties too. They ate like kings in those days.

The euphoria had not returned, and hardly any of the food had been eaten over the last five months. Soon after his supermarket spree, he had started closing down the shop. He had the phone stopped after two irritating calls in a single day, one from a firm in Hyannis offering to manage his money, and one offering more life insurance. He had paid his electricity bill for six months, made a further down payment for regular visits of the oil truck to the fuel line out on the road for his pathetic boiler, and then stopped paying anything else, and stopped going out to shop. The mail would all be sent to their apartment in New York, which they had kept; his former graduate assistant lived there now and knew better than to disturb him. It began to seem too difficult to engage with the practical world at all. He could not now see past the images crowding in on him, or fathom the forms of any outside world, and he certainly could not move at its pace.

Bear down, he told himself: make an inventory. Looking through the cabinets he found he still had plenty of food left, staples as well as luxuries—perhaps enough for four weeks. He reckoned that would take him into the third week of March. Perhaps spring would come early after all. He made an inventory of everything that was left under the various categories of food, and was now in a position to add a second rule to old Rule Four: Plan, cook, and eat balanced and nutritious meals once a day. He drew up sequences of menus that he thought might conform to this rule, though waffles, bacon, maple syrup, and orange juice reappeared many times in the week.

Now he had to answer the question of what sort of work he would do. There was a path beckoning him, but it took him a while to see it straight. Eventually he was able to write: "On the few occasions when you come to yourself, and are not seeing visions or dreaming dreams, you are forced to realize that you are clenched tight as a fist. The rage seems to be threefold—at the incompleteness of things, that however hard you take stock, nothing tallies to a total; and at the fact that you are no longer your own person, thinking your own thoughts, but increasingly the prey of random images that assault you; and at the fact, most important, that you were robbed long before the end of people you loved, and powers you had, and always pointlessly. The work you do should respond to all these furies: Tell a story to its end.

"The first thing is to get yourself in shape to stop unbidden pictures—call them hallucinations—from coursing through your mind. Eat more, and make yourself stronger, and perhaps you'll have more control over the direction your thoughts take. (Bless me, Father, for I have sinned: my mind teems with siren thoughts. Do you entertain them, my son? No, but by God, they entertain me.) This will not do. Steal a march on the random images that invade you, by choosing and filling the mind with the pictures you will attend to; drive them together with strong connections into a story you can't take your mind off. Teller of tales, do not wait to be possessed; start building a seamless construction, impregnable to daydreams. When you go to bed, of course, you'll have to take whatever dreams are sent, and maybe some will be of use. The theme doesn't matter much, though you should avoid the morose, half-lit, underworld scenes, which sap your vitals. Pick something that offers you a quick line into action that will possess you."

MacIver thought he saw his way clearer and drafted a companion for Rule Seven: "Work to consist of telling a story <u>to the end, not just shards, but the whole pot.</u>"

Now he read the revised rules over. He did not particularly like what he termed "their pissy, hectoring tone," but he had to admit he had it coming to him. Now he would take hold, nudging the words, the thoughts, the pictures into necessary connections; the undisciplined storm of images, which had bludgeoned him into a helpless spectator, would now, he hoped, be channeled aside by the advancing wedge of his coherent story.

On the whole he felt he had brought some order and resolve to his abject life. These were tough, good rules—tough but fair. He went back to the original draft and inserted his new subsets as separate rules on burning, eating, and working in the appropriate places. He retabulated them all and found that he now had a list of ten. The number pleased him, and he went back to the top of the page, and under its heading squeezed in another subtitle—Ten Commandments for Old Men Waiting. Play up and play the game.

CHAPTER 2

Hatching the Plot

For the first time in a long while, MacIver went to bed that night in some anticipation of the next day. He kept thinking about what he should write. His mind was drawn back to the mental film he had stored of the athletic soldiers making their way with such dash across the open terrain: perhaps he should just follow them and see where they led him. But he was wary of them for his theme, for various reasons. The first, of course, was that he had just resolved to keep a lid on the unbidden dreams and visions, by actually taking hold and shaping and choosing the images that he would attend to by himself; to hell with all this feverish suggestibility. But there were two other reasons that the soldiers did not ring exactly true for him—one was the scale of their operation, all movements concerted, all participants anonymous, the corps de ballet in khaki. His sense was that he should choose a smaller cast, and make particular characters, sharply individual, that he could be interested in. The other false note, from where he stood, in the running and cutting soldiers was an arrogant, triumphalist tone pervading the whole: MacIver, given where he was now headed, was not at all sure he would tell a tale of victory. In his professional life, he had been a historian of World War I, and had achieved some success with his first book, *Voices Through the Smoke*, which had examined the policy background, the production in Britain and Canada, and the long-term effects of the use of poison gas. There had been a lot of detail in the book, but from the public's point of view the most compelling part had been the interviews he had conducted with 137 victims of poison gas lingering in hospitals and nursing homes around the country some fourteen years after the event. The book was considered one of the earliest and most powerful uses of oral history, and was correctly read as an angry young man's work; in a series of ugly vignettes it tore strips off the false sentiment, and false optimism, attending that starchy, fumbling, brutal war.

But the book contained, as always, only a sample of all he had heard and seen while researching it. Over time, the rage had banked down to a slow burn, yet his mind was still well stocked with images and voices: he thought he would use some of them to write a story about a particular sector of the front in a short span of time. (He did not expect to have too much time himself.) He would assemble a small cast of characters, pop them into a trench in Flanders, and describe how they worked on each other, and how the large events worked on them. He could not see the end right now, but it would come to him.

He woke several times in the night, with the curious mix of chills and night sweats that had beset him recently, and after turning the pillow over to find a dry spot, lay there thinking with some excitement about what he would write. As the night wore on, he thought he had found a quiet way into his story. But he stayed awake, now relaxedly and comfortably, and found himself playing, for the first time in quite a long time, with his memories of his father. There was not, actually, a whole lot to remember. He had vivid memories of Loch Affric and his boyhood there in the highlands of Scotland, but most of the detailed pictures of his father were of his departures from the place.

His father had moved the two of them, his mother and himself, there from London in 1915, while he went off to fly for the Royal Flying Corps in France, imposing a wonderful idyll on his young son, and the bleakest isolation on his wife; it also lengthened his own travel time home on leave by several hours. MacIver wondered afterwards why he had done it. Certainly there was no risk for them in London in that war. He was inclined to think that his father was positioning them at this critical juncture in his life to indulge his own romantic streak: Alastair MacIver was every inch a highlander himself, and as he put his life at risk up in the air in those flimsy machines, he wanted to think of his loved ones up in those sparsely peopled glens—it achieved a concentration of sentiment, as it were. Lately his son wondered whether the punitive action to remove his mother from harm's way had been prompted by his father's anxiety to keep her faithful. He was perhaps an unreasonably possessive man, and she certainly did love London; they moved back there very soon after he was killed, when the war was still mired in the trenches. But by then the boy was a dyed-in-the-tartan Scot himself, and *that* was probably what his father had intended.

So most of his wartime memories of his father were of his leaving—their good-byes, never of course with any thought that one of them would be the last ("Will you get killed, Father?" "No, Robert, I'm very lucky—I get to fly in the good clean air, while all the poor soldiers have to slog it out in horrible mud"), and somehow more memorable, the stagy farewells to his mother at the front door on Sunday nights, observed from the landing on the stairs after bedtime. The tall figure in the bulky service coat enveloping his quiet wife; the door closing, the sound of the station Daimler purring away to silence down the track behind the house, and then the distracted sounds of his mother's tidying up downstairs, living room being straightened, sherry glasses into the sink.

And then there was the last farewell. For the funeral they got to ride in the Daimler themselves. The service and burial were at the little stone church at the end of the lake on a raw, clear day in April. They were well attended, with many of his own friends, the sons of gillies and crofters, there straight from school, and the airmen of his father's squadron strongly represented in uniform, looking seasoned warriors to Robert, but, as the local newspaper photograph showed, just boys themselves. At the burial in the churchyard overlooking the loch, there was an RFC bugler for the Last Post, and at the end up on the hill behind them a piper from Captain MacIver's clan played one of the dark highland laments. While it was still in the air around them, the sergeant in charge of the honor guard brought him his father's fleece-lined flying jacket, a voluminous, weighty thing, beautifully made.

"Your father would want you to have this—you'll grow into it in no time, son," he said kindly.

"Thank you, sir," said Robert. "Do you know if he came down in the mud, when they shot his plane down?"

The man looked startled, but gathered himself. "Yes, I'm afraid he did," he said evenly.

"He would have hated that," Robert said sadly.

But in the car going back to the house with his mother, he burst out angrily, "He said he wouldn't get killed!" She was looking out the window, watching the lake go by, but he thought he heard a sigh. "Yes, darling, he said that to me, too," she said. After that, he played all the schoolboy games, both out in the wild and on the playing fields between the chalk-marked lines, with such fierce abandon that even his teammates feared him.

MacIver finally dropped into two hours of undisturbed sleep, but was up at six-fifteen, before dawn on another freezing February day. He made toast and tea for breakfast, shaved, and made his bed. He was at his desk as the pale morning light started to explore the pictures on the far wall, his legal pad and old Waterman pen in front of him. He had decided he would begin in longhand, and then move to his trusty Smith Corona if he felt he had a run going. He sat for a few moments composing himself, slightly hunched under his faded Wasps rugby cap, dressing gown tied over his blue fisherman's sweater and baggy crap-catcher corduroys, tartan rug over his knees, arthritic old feet stuffed into two pairs of Wigwam sweat socks and down-at-heel slippers. He had tried to honor his Australian tutor's "Helpful hints for Sydney ex-servicemen, on successful exam-taking"—head cool, feet warm, bowels clear. Well, at least his head was cool, even under the cap. Little by little, he brought himself to focus, his hands resting on the oak in front of him, still strong despite the knobby knuckles and the archipelago of liver spots running across the back of them. Then he picked up his pen, and wrote out the invocation he had composed during the night. The idea was to put some words on the page straight off, so the storyteller would not be intimidated by its bareness.

"I said to my soul, Be still, and watch the small trickling beginnings ease towards flood. Let the story declare itself, and the characters and events take me down among them and draw the words out of me. I have tried to possess my soul in patience, I have gathered all the hungers of my past in readiness, to spell out all the missing syllables of my life. In the morning watch I shall wait, and the quick, brown, wordy fox will come out of his hole, sniff the air, and begin his narration. It is only natural. Sooner or later, if I watch, it is bound to happen. Then I shall fill my book with profitable wonders."

But he didn't have forever. He had decided he would begin populating his Flanders trench with a baddie, to whom he had given the name of Braddis. He took his legal pad and wrote at the top: "Sergeant Braddis cleans his nails." Here is what he wrote the first day:

Tuesday afternoon after tea. As always at this time, Reggie Braddis sat on the fire-step cleaning his nails, before a few interested and sycophantic observers. Actually, the ritual began with the filing and oiling of his bayonet, whose top three inches he kept razor sharp on both sides, and about half the regulation width. Sometimes it was just a matter of a few loving strokes with the file, and testing its edge by slicing the oily cloth with which he anointed it; but on other occasions, the week's work had broken the point, and he would have to start to replicate the edge lower down. Even when this had happened, Braddis would always wait until Tuesday before repairing his bayonet: he liked conveying the impression of military ritual and order. No one had ever witnessed the work which had damaged the bayonet, because it was always done in no-man's-land in the middle of the night. Sergeant Braddis would earlier lead out the regular patrols and wire parties, but after he had brought them back he would go out again on his own. He seemed to need no sleep at all. There was enough excitement in the regular business of war, and in the license it gave him for irregular business of his own, to keep his adrenaline pumped at all times. On these later, solitary sallies, he would not take his rifle with him—only the bayonet in its sheath, and a couple of booby-trap bombs he prepared from mortar shells on Friday afternoons at the same time. There were many unsavory legends, which he did nothing to discourage, about his solitary exploits in no-man's-land, or Braddis Land, as he liked to call it.

After attending to the bayonet, he would turn to his nails, specifically the thumbnail and middle fingernail of both hands. All four of these nails were grown to a length of a fairly precise three quarters of an inch from the end of the finger, and all shaped to a point very close to the lines of the bayonet, though unlike the bayonet, they seemed to be preternaturally strong, and no one had ever seen one of them broken. The sergeant manicured them fastidiously in two stages, first using the point of the bayonet to remove the smallest trace of dirt, then its razor side to pare the nails back to standard length, and then a small nail file to restore the sharpness all around. Groups of men in his platoon would watch this intimate process in the hopes of seeing one of the periodic demonstrations Braddis gave of his nails in action. Once, for example, just after he had completed the manicure to his satisfaction, he noticed a large rat scurrying along one of the few dry parts of the trench, sticking close to the wall. He moved well for such a powerful man, and in a moment had leapt and landed with his full weight on the rat's back, behind its front legs. The rat's spine had been broken and its back legs crushed by Braddis's weight. In one easy motion, he stooped and picked up the broken animal, not much shorter than his boot. A thin squeal emerged with blood from its thrashing mouth. Braddis drove the middle fingernail and thumbnail of his left hand into the small bright eyes and on into the brain.

One more spasm and the rat hung limp. Braddis lobbed it over the wall of the trench, and said quietly, "You see—they work for rats and they work for Huns, too." The men were not inclined to doubt him. Images of those nails closing like the teeth of a trap on some German jugular in the dark, and then ripping it out without a sound, colored all their thoughts of their sergeant.

But the nails were capable of more delicate work. Once when Private Tim Callum, whom he hated for his quiet detachment, was working on a sketch farther down the trench, paying no attention to the Tuesday manicure, Braddis noticed him and walked slowly down and stood behind him, looking over his shoulder. Callum never looked up, but Braddis leant forward and tore the drawing off the sketch pad, and held it up in his right hand. "I never let anyone draw me without permission," he said, and proceeded to slice it into strips, using only the outside edge of his left thumbnail. "I wasn't drawing you, Sergeant," said Callum quietly, looking straight ahead into the wall of the trench. "Could have fooled me," said Braddis with a short laugh. "You can't be too careful."

As with many of his type, Braddis enjoyed the fear and fascination that his dangerous unpredictability instilled in his men. Soon after the Callum incident, perhaps because he had thought there might be some secret sympathy for the private, he turned the Tuesday ritual against himself. When everything had been done as meticulously as ever, he stood up dramatically, his eyes shut in an expression of great concentration, his fists clenched tightly in front of him. Soon blood started dripping quite steadily off the closed hands. He stood there perfectly still until someone said urgently, to break the spell, "You're bleeding, Sarge," at which Braddis slowly spread his arms wide, and then opened his hands, so that they could all see the deep incisions his middle fingernails had made in both palms. The blood streamed off them, onto the duckboards and into the mud for another half-minute or so, and then Braddis opened his eyes and said: "You see, I have the Christ-wounds. I am a holy man, a crazy fucking barbarian saint, doing the Lord's work for my country."

He bandaged his hands himself, and never lost a moment's duty. These were some of the ways the sergeant ensured that the war stood close to them all in the trench at all times, even on quiet days. He knew he would be doomed if normal life and normal judgments were allowed to settle for an instant.

MacIver was satisfied with Braddis: it was clear he would be nothing but trouble. The question was whether he could imagine anyone strong enough to hold his own against him. He tidied up a bit, and then thought about supper. Tonight he would be serving pasta, with broccoli and San Marzano tomatoes. Margaret, even out of such simplicity (but did he remember these ingredients with fresh scallops added?), would make a delicious seamless composition whose various parts all seemed to cohere and enhance each other. The house would fill with anticipatory smells and when he came to the table, he would find in a beautiful stoneware bowl an effortlessly harmonious dish, whose colors alone conjured up the Italian flag. Of course, her ingredients were fresh, though she did use those canned tomatoes, draining some of the juice so as not to produce too much slop, and then enhancing flavors and smells by cooking them with chopped shallots, a little olive oil. He didn't have any shallots, but he didn't see why he couldn't achieve a near miss with a basic onion.

This time, instead of spooking him, his reenactment of these observed rituals induced a kind of wistful calm. The truth was, he was a little pleased with himself: you felt better if you did something—anything—and since he had been jolted by his fall into establishing a new rhythm to fill his remaining days, it seemed to have unlocked his frozen resentment against the end-that-would-not-come. He even felt warmer. He ate his dinner slowly and started working through his first bottle of Meursault, raising his glass to the end of time; it all tasted good. Then he cleaned up carefully and, to keep the mellow mood flowing, put on the slow movement of Mahler's Sixth Symphony, an old favorite.

With his glass refilled, he sat in his rocking chair and listened as the theme, at first slackly toned, headed off gently downhill, apparently going nowhere, a dog peeing in snow. But then a little development and a period of agitation, from which the theme emerged striding more confidently and briskly, cellos digging into the chords and bracing them. A climax built: the violins soared to a piercing sweetness, and then swooped once more buoyantly downhill with other strings rising to meet and cross them: it always reminded him of the best broken-field running. Poor bloody neurasthenic Mahler, with his migraines and his sad premonitory songs spelling death for his children—who would have thought he could be such an athlete in his mind?

Not for the first time, he allowed the music to revive some glory moments of his own. Scotland vs. England at Twickenham—a still grey January afternoon and sixty-five thousand noisy fans in the stands. Ten minutes to go with England leading 9–6. Scotland had had its chances and a good supply of the ball, but the fly-half Stewart had kept wasting it by keeping it himself and cutting straight back into the pursuit—a death wish for obliteration. MacIver had spoken to him firmly about it at halftime, but nothing had changed. Once or twice young Colin Cameron on the wing had picked up a loose ball and shown his pace with high-stepping runs, but he had been cut down each time. You had to hand it to this English side, baying like foxhounds to each other in their overbred voices, they were bloody quick.

It was time to make a move. Sure enough, the ball came out on the Scottish side once more, and Stewart, instead of passing, kept it and turned inside for the inevitable tackle. This time, MacIver, crossing to clear the loose ball, and with the fly-half still on the ground, landed with his studs and full fourteen stone on the back of his teammate's knee. As he pushed off, gathered the ball, and kicked it out of play, he heard a satisfying yell of pain. In the age before substitutions were allowed, Stewart, badly hobbled, was sent out to the wing. In the press box, the radio announcer had described the incident as "one of those unfortunate accidents generated by the sheer pace of the game," but the same man in the bar after the game had looked MacIver straight in the eye and said matter-of-factly: "Ruthless bugger, aren't you? Good for you."

But the clock was now edging towards injury time. MacIver put the other center at fly-half, and told him to open it up. It took them a couple of minutes to find a rhythm with this correction, but then the heroic forwards yet again fed them the ball from the line-out, about ten yards inside the Scottish half. A quick long serve from Gordon to Morrison, and the ball was MacIver's. He took it at full stride and turned on the burners, straining for the outside. It might be that the English had grown too accustomed to Stewart's inside break, or simply tired in the waning minutes. By the time the pursuit had adjusted, it had to look for an angle on him downfield. Reach for it, MacIver told himself, sear those lungs. He continued to strain for the outside, watching the English coverage stretching itself out. Then almost on a syncopated note, he planted his left foot, and cut back the other way. Boom!—BOOM! The body of the big English wing-forward Jarvis passed in front of his as he made his cut. Straightaway he was in the clear; the fullback David was over-committed to his right, and MacIver drove up the middle, all, it seemed, on one breath, to score under the posts. Before the movement began, he had been feeling sluggish, but the adrenaline pumped him up again, and the line came up to meet him almost too fast to relish the moment. He remembered the English crowd falling silent under the shock of this turn of events: 9–9, and the kick to follow. His friend John Wilson, the Scottish full-back and kicker, came up to make the conversion, businesslike as always, and said, "I don't intend to waste anything that good." The careful placement of the ball, the poised stance at the start of the approach, the smack of leather being squarely struck amid total silence, and then the sight of the ball soaring high straight between the posts. Scotland beats England 11–9 in the waning moments of the game.

The *Sunday Express* the next morning had a panoramic photograph of the field with MacIver making his cut, under the headline X MARKS THE SPOT!!! The amazing reflexes of the sports photographer had caught the instant at which, with every other player leaning leftwards, MacIver's body alone slants right, and Jarvis's body passing across his in the middle of the picture completes a perfect *X*. He still had the photograph somewhere. It had been a long time after that before anyone in Scotland would let him buy his own single malt. But the best thing of all was that the next match the selectors had dropped Stewart.

MacIver felt better about things. He put his wine glass in the sink and shuffled off to bed, thinking smugly to himself, "You used to be quite quick."

CHAPTER 3

Characters

He had been a little too cocky there, and he'd paid for it during the night. Suddenly, his illness had woken up and decided to assert itself. It was as though it had been decreed, "Here is this absurd person fooling around with his imagination and his memory of this and that, and it's certainly time to show him what a fact is." He had been woken up by fierce stabs of pain in his left side, but well below the heart, he realized, and rising tides of nausea. Eventually he knew he would have to get to the bathroom in record time, if he was not to face a foul clean-up problem in the morning. He only just made it. Torrents of vomit erupted from him painfully in repeated waves into the basin, his eyes tearing and the sweat pouring off him with the effort. He could see enough to discern that there was blood and bile and some white matter in the mix. When it was all spent, and the taps had managed to wash all but splash traces of it down the sink, he washed his face and brushed his teeth to remove the horrible taste, and stripped naked to towel off the sweat. He had been bent over, and knew instinctively that he should stand up very carefully; he was in fact still trembling all over.

He left the light on in the bathroom in case there was to be a second performance, and went back to the bedroom for some clean clothes. Passing the wardrobe mirror, he now noticed that in addition to his small regular paunch (really just a trifle of sag in the gut, if you were being kind), he was now sporting a pronounced and asymmetric swelling on the left side of his belly. He was beginning to get the picture: as was the case with the decadent Roman Empire, the point is reached when there is no organic unity of the whole; the provinces all start to go their own way, to break away and form their allegiances elsewhere, or sometimes to mass malignant forces at the frontier, and at the right moment erupt and begin an advance against the soft center. Not for nothing did the generals keep looking to drive against the soft underbelly. This was what was happening to him amidships.

He was back in bed now in a clean sweatshirt, underwear, and sweatpants, still feeling frail and slightly atremble, but without the nausea and with the fierce stabbing in his side reduced to a subdued, metronomic pricking. Few inner gratitudes run deeper than the one that greets release from violent pain. He lay quietly, considering whether he had done anything to induce this attack. No, he decided, he knew it had been down there biding its time. The question was whether he should now formally repudiate wine, to use the awful, medical phrase, *just to be safe.*

Hell, no, his naturally rebellious soul declared, slimily adding a little quote from Saint Paul to Timothy, "Take a little wine for your stomach's sake." Aha!

He was up before dawn as usual, and sipped two or three glasses of water first: he seemed to have lost gallons of liquid in the night. Then he made himself hot tea with honey and lemon, swallowed a passel of vitamins, and was able to eat half an English muffin and marmalade on top of that. Then he went back to work. MacIver had fashioned a bad person to lead off his story, and should imagine a good one now to balance him. He found him in a gamekeeper on a Norfolk estate.

Charles Alston
GAMEKEEPER

Charles Alston sat blocky in his greatcoat, face painted solid red by the firelight, both hands around his tea mug. He was telling them about animal behavior on the estate at Blickling. It was pleasant for him to tell the stories, pulling him back to the exact site of each encounter; and it was good of them, he thought, to listen to him so quietly, and let him get away from all this. He supposed they each had somewhere to go in their minds, but now they were letting him go to his place instead. "Now the badger," he was saying, staring into the fire, "is a very quiet, clean, and decent animal, who keeps pretty much to himself. He digs his burrow in the ground (you call it a sett, you know, for badgers) and has several rooms or chambers in it. He keeps it all immaculate. The straw and soft leaves he takes down for bedding he won't just leave there. He will replace it regular to keep it fresh. And he wouldn't dream of going to the toilet in his bedchamber. But the fox on the other hand is a handsome cocky fellow all right, and he's got a good head on him, but he's lazy and very dirty, too. He smells awful rank. The fox often can't be bothered to dig himself a hole, he's got too much going on, or he never gets around to it, so sometimes he'll just move into the badger's den. He just up and moves right in, without so much as a knock on the door. Now the interesting thing is that the badger could take the fox on, if he had a mind to, and really punish him. He's brave as a lion, and he's very low-slung and powerful with an underthrust, and he's got teeth that will clamp like a steel trap and never release. But once the fox has set foot in his place, the badger will always just walk away from it. Can't stand the smell of it anymore, you see, that awful fox smell. If he knew how to fumigate it, he probably would, but as it is he would much rather start over, nice and clean again, than have to breathe in that fox-stench. It's strange, but that's the way it is. It's a wonder that the fox doesn't take advantage of that all the time, but he probably doesn't realize how bad he smells. He's got used to it himself and rather likes it."

MacIver saw no need to push this any further on the day. Tomorrow he would try to introduce young Simon Dodds, the subaltern in command of the platoon. In the meantime, he wanted to think some more. He had met quite a few solid, decent Alstons, the best of East Anglia, when he was developing his oral history archive on the war; he wanted his sample of four or five from a platoon on the front to be close to what he knew. Admittedly, he had met only two possible Braddises who had survived the war: it was fortunate they were rare, but he needed one of them for his story. But the whole exercise of finding these people was bringing him back to the long series of encounters he had had when he was trying to bring the war close to himself for the purposes of history.

In the meantime, there was supper to attend to, and he thought with relief that this aspect of the Rules would now prove easier than he had feared; surely on last night's performance he qualified for invalid rations, which, without weaseldom, meant he could go back to eating less rather than more. For supper tonight he had two slices of bacon, a slice of seven-grain toast with strawberry jam, and two glasses of warm water, with which everything seemed to go down a little easier. After supper he listened to Mozart, *Marriage of Figaro,* Acts Three and Four, beginning with the duet *Che soave zefiretto,* the two women sending in turn the lovely ripples of their voices gently chasing across the limpid pool. Whatever Mozart's follies, he knew women and he never left them out.

MacIver sat on, after the lovely hymnlike *Ah! Tutti contenti* and the merry scramble to the finish, now in a relaxed and quietly somber frame of mind, and let his thoughts run over his personal register of fallen heroes. They kept coming back to linger, for no particular reason, on one of his gas victims, Ben Winterbourne, whose interview he could put his hand on in seconds, thanks to Margaret's quiet insistence. Years ago, at a critical stage, she had bought him a fine old oak filing cabinet, after coming upon his innumerable folders crammed into shelves in apparently random order, yellowing and drooping with neglect. The section on gas interviews was now in the top drawer, and had been put into alphabetical order, at first by Margaret, hoping to shame him into some activity. She had succeeded eventually, when, sitting beside her as she worked, he started thumbing through some of them, and finally realized that they were full of vivid details, that the men's sufferings made his insignificant, and that his record of them constituted a memorial to them that ought to be decently preserved. He thanked her, apologized gravely, and took over the work of filing from the letter *D.* Now on an impulse, he went to the cabinet. The drawer slid out on its smooth runners, and there, properly under *W,* was Ben, Research Case 113, Watling Nursing Home, Chatham, Kent. He ran through the details—born April 26, 1898, Herne Bay, Kent. Signed on East Kent Regiment (the Buffs) July 2, 1916. Still a private at time of injury, Messines, Ypres salient, May 14, 1917.

Then a complicated series of shuttles from field hospitals, and through England. Interviewed April 10 and May 3, 1932. He put the file back and returned to his chair.

MacIver remembered the interviews perfectly. Nondescript Victorian nursing home outside Chatham. Big, bare, sightless windows set in grey stucco, overlooking a neglected garden, rank hydrangeas beneath ground-floor windows, plantain weeds and dock leaves winning out over grass on the lawn; a monkey puzzle tree on one side of the path, and quite a respectable cedar on the other. A house that had grown used to being unvisited. It reinforced MacIver's notion that the medical people made a point of parking these gas victims in backwaters where they would be out of sight. BW's room on first floor overlooking the front. The blind was torn, and an old army blanket had been tacked on top of it to give him some extra shade. His eyes still very weak. Two black oxygen cylinders on the floor, and on the metal bedside table a black rubber mask with the hose attached, an enamel bowl with a cloth over it for him to spit into, and a couple of well-thumbed sports magazines. Sometimes with these people his rugby had been a help.

Ben in bed when he arrived, small figure, you would have thought a young teenager, humped facing the window. When he sat up, sickness and premature aging quite evident. Thin mousy hair receding, and much scrofula on scalp, pink-rimmed eyes with exaggerated dark pouches underneath, pink-rimmed nostrils also on narrow nose pointing upwards, as though under pressure from buckteeth below. Halfway, you might say, on his way to being a sick albino rat. Under the green surgical gown, pitifully thin arms without muscle, and concave, permanently wheezy chest.

"Hello, Ben."

"You again. I thought I'd sent you packing."

"*Fuck off* were the words you used. The Sister was mortified."

"Yeah"—with a chuckle. "That wasn't nice."

"So feeling better, are you?"

"Depends what for."

"I want to talk to you."

"About the fuckin' war?"

"Yes, about the fucking war, and before the war and after the war."

Last time, to his fury, MacIver had lost the small ferrety man by letting him run on about his boyhood. Before he knew it, the hard edge of bitterness had been softened by the act of reminiscing. BW started to remember the tough little tyke he had been, full of merriment and mischief—you never knew what he'd get up to next. As he told the old stories, they brought him home to the forbidden ground of what he had lost and how he had changed. Now his anger had poisoned all relationships, no one could be put in the two empty beds in the room, and not even his long-suffering sister could abide him in her house. He had hardened himself in the corrosive toxins, and needed the bitterness to keep going; but here, talking himself back into the world of lost possibilities, he could feel himself being undone. Much more of this and he might cry in front of this persistently probing stranger, who was making him go slower to get down to the details. That could not be endured.

In his anxiety, he had started yelling at MacIver, and brought on a coughing fit. Clouds of purple rose to his face, eyes bulging with the strain of the spasms, and then a sudden lurch to the covered bowl to retch into it. MacIver wanted to hold him, but was sure that if he added one more jot to his rage, he would finish him off. Fortunately, a nurse arrived to investigate the noise.

But Ben had not finished with him. "Do you want to see, MacIver?" he had shouted between gasps, clutching the bowl with both hands, robe wrenched off his knobby shoulders, sweat and tears streaming down the flushed face. "Do you want to see how the yellow gets mixed with the red?" Holding the bowl up to him.

"It's all right, Ben," MacIver said quietly. "I've seen it."

The anger had spent itself. The voice now quiet and tired. "You see, MacIver," he said in patient explanation to an equal, "I got all my roads and pathways blocked. Things fall into 'em, you see, scrapings, like rust in a drain."

"That's how it must be, Ben. I'll leave you to rest, and come back later."

"That's right, MacIver. You fuck off."

In fact, it hadn't been easy to get another appointment. The nursing home didn't want visitors upsetting their patients. They only relented when Winterbourne himself kept asking for him. This time, MacIver promised the Sister and vowed to himself, he would concentrate on the war and its aftermath. Enough on the bloody boyhood.

BW had had one experience of poison gas, before his fatal encounter. The first time, his platoon was entrenched at Passchendaele; mustard gas had been released off to the northeast; they had news of it over the radio, and were told to put on gas masks, because the wind would carry it down towards them; then the wind veered and carried the gas farther east, and after a while the all clear was given. "But even the order to put on the masks produced a pretty fair panic; some blokes felt suffocated just wearing the awful things, and some of us would relieve our own fright by preyin' on them, loomin' up sudden with those monster insect faces, so they had fits. Of course, you couldn't tell foe from friend wearin' that fuckin' mask. I can remember one poor bugger ripped his off, just so he could be free to scream. You should've seen his 'orrible contorted face."

The next time was for real. BW's section had been sent out as a wire party into no-man's-land. Quiet summer night, big guns quiet, not really dark enough. Most of them hadn't even taken their masks with them; they had enough to carry, what with tools and bales of the lethal barbed wire, without that "edgy, bouncing box" around their necks. They never heard the cough of the mortars that lobbed two canisters smack into the middle of the section as it was grouped around a large artillery crater. It seemed nobody moved for a full minute. "It was as though we was frozen starin' at two huge snakes lying there hissin' at us. Then someone screamed Gas! at the top of his voice—you could've heard it in Brighton—and most of them started running like hell back to our lines. That was the whole fuckin' point of it of course. The machine guns were waiting. Jerry sent up a flare, to show him what he was doing, and mowed down most of my friends right there in the open, lucky sods." They didn't mow down Ben: he couldn't run, because he couldn't see. "I was crawlin' in and out of craters like a fuckin' mole with acid in its eyes."

They moved on to the casualty station—the care was brisk but very good. Everything seemed to confirm MacIver's thesis that the farther from the battlefield the patient got, the more offhand, the less professional, the attention became, and the more distant the event in time, the more dismissive, and the more shaded-to-denial the official attitude dealing with it. MacIver remembered the mustachioed brigadier from the medical corps who finally in 1932 granted him an interview after much badgering from a sympathetic MP MacIver had enlisted. The man would clearly not have made it to even the middle ranks of the medical profession, and he had decided to try his hand at a soldierly persona instead; it had paid off for him, so he had driven on to complete a parody of the most Blimpish soldier: "People die in war, goddammit, but there's no reason why they shouldn't die well turned out" had been MacIver's favorite line (spoken about the medic's view that slovenly dress in the trenches had led to serious indiscipline and demoralization).

The brigadier sat ramrod straight, uniformed and bemedaled, just enough grey in the black hair to make it steely and senior, rather flushed, whether from the presence of MacIver or high blood pressure he could not diagnose. Square hands with tidy nails, and black hair on the back of them; they rested on the table on their sides, with one curled around the back of the other, and moved in tandem with minimal gestures up and down, two inches the maximum liftoff allowed for emphasis. The only strategy in the conversation, it emerged, was to maintain the official double-line intact, whatever artillery MacIver brought against it. The two facts, which any decent, reasonable man would grant immediately, were that every conceivable care had been taken of the gas victims, and that the whole episode had been blown out of proportion: "No, professor," he said with weary disdain, "I'm afraid there's a lot of mythology about this gas business. Of course, everyone's afraid of what they can't see. But really the gas played a pretty insignificant role: of all the disabilities after the war, only 2 percent were gas related. More than 60 percent of those were cured within seven weeks of their incident, more than 80 percent released from hospital, if you push it up to nine weeks. There is not a single case of death later than the eighth week from gassing. So in my view all the public agitation and Geneva protocols have made a mountain out of a molehill. I blame that painter fellow Sargent for some of the mass hysteria. I can't believe the Imperial War Museum actually displays his picture to the public. Goddamn dilettante Yankee painter drives out to the front, visits a casualty station after tea, and goes home to paint columns of young soldiers with bandaged eyes, all in a drab mustard color, all playing blindman's bluff, as they're led through countless droves of sprawling comrades, all similarly afflicted. Gives a totally inflated view. If I had my way, I'd have burnt the damn painting."

"Yes, I've read the medical reports, too," MacIver said shortly. "But I have also visited 137 veterans of the war in nursing homes of one kind or another, whose lives have been permanently blighted by an incident with gas at least fourteen years ago."

"Almost certainly," the brigadier replied, trying to claim some medical high ground against this Commie academic, "these are the effects of neurasthenia interacting with a previous bronchial or asthmatic condition."

It had got uglier after that. MacIver put the memory aside, and thought more about his platoon. There would be no gas casualties with this lot—he had seen too many of those already. But on average, he supposed, every platoon was likely to contain a spunky little tyke like Ben Winterbourne, not particularly good or bad, but as they say in the official character reports, "easily led." MacIver played with this phrase for some minutes before going to sleep; it usually wore a negative connotation, implying "following unhealthy influences to no good end," which he supposed meant following the line of least resistance, "unchecked by any principles of his own." But why should the phrase always wear this negative aspect? A man like Alston would be easily led, in the sense that he would stay with you, follow your mind, and when the situation called for some initiative on his own, he would see what had to be done, not necessarily like lightning but effectively, maybe better than you would, and do it in good order. In the very brief period of his own command, MacIver remembered, he had been blessed with a whole crew trained to such discipline; the moments that had called for precise, prompt action can have amounted in sum to only a handful of minutes, but MacIver had been so disappointed that it came to an end, he now realized, that he had never really acknowledged how lucky he had been.

CHAPTER 4

The Young Star-Captains

Health bulletin on Professor MacIver: the patient spent a restless but tolerable night without any of the disgusting manifestations of the previous one. Still, there was pain, but bearable, and a fever that seemed to rise and fall in the course of the night—he rode its swales up and down, near the higher crests feeling light-headed and fearing a return of his delusions, but he held on; night sweats aplenty, and after the worst of them it was hard to find a dry place in the pillows or sheets. However, he was up before dawn, forcing himself to eat the now standard bit of seven-grain toast, the swallowing eased again with warm water, which he again followed with the chaser of tea with honey and lemon. His St. John's Ambulance first aid course had recommended "warm, sweet tea" as a treatment for shock (at least for British patients); MacIver was not feeling particularly shocked, but those people had run an empire, so it couldn't have hurt. And now he was ready for work.

Lieutenant Simon Dodds
PLATOON COMMANDER

Simon Dodds was a born subaltern; by class and by the precise average of his talents and bearing, he could not be stationed much lower, and by the same criteria he was not likely, in any normal set of circumstances, to rise much higher—which MacIver knew was a pity. Soft brown hair and soft brown eyes and a soft full mouth, with a good straight nose between them— the whole impression left was of a genial slack passivity, a friendly animal going about his humdrum life halfway up the food chain, certainly no predator and not much of a prey. The strange thing was that a swift impression offered a slight resemblance to his sergeant, Reggie Braddis. They could have come out of the same Norfolk gene pool, though Braddis's life and inner demons had hardened him and prepared him for tougher games, forcing the bone closer to the skin, the mind into tighter knots of calculation.

There seemed nothing tough about Dodds. He was the son of a Church of England vicar in a poor East Anglian village, a forgotten church for an abstracted man, whose thoughts streamed as airy and unengaged as the Norfolk clouds passing overhead. His father viewed his son, his only child, with benign puzzlement and a sense that it would be an act of arrogance to expect much from him. The mother, a sweet woman, worked with nervous worry to anchor down some details in her husband's simple life. The boy, by Vagueness out of Dither, turned out placid. He moved indistinctly, with hardly a bow wave, through the village school and on to a lesser public school. He was no trouble to anyone else, and seemed to trouble himself very little with whatever work was expected of him; he got by, but mastery was not within his horizon. He sent from school no signals of passion or curiosity out into the world, and so left his teachers with the impression that he was dull and self-contained.

Which was a true impression, unless you moved him to a different world—the world where boats are sailed on water. To see Simon Dodds at the tiller of his spanking fourteen-foot dinghy, the *Windrush,* beating up the Broads and catching the last breath of air to offset the turn of the tide, was to see a different animal altogether, a knowing, engaged citizen of the curling byways of the Flatlands. Here the gates of his senses were open and alert to every changing impression. His nose scented the precise degrees of mud and salt in the inchmeal gains of land and sea against each other. He saw the slices of shadow off the banks darkening the water and cutting off its corners, and heard the first breath of the evening breeze rattle the reeds, and the last call of the bittern going to bed. This world was his, the whole geography of the place, with its huge sky and grudging threads of water, and the strange abrupt landmarks thrown up apparently always out of place behind the sedge: the sawn-off church tower, the windmill sails bodiless, each one suggesting by its dislocation that you can't get there from here. In such a world you learn patience and humility, you take what the even tug of sheet and tiller gives you; and when you know the channels as well as Simon Dodds, you accept that sooner or later, if you let it lead you, the river will tilt its way out of sight and become the main thoroughfare of a lost old village becalmed, where a little jetty is offered for your mooring, and you can stretch your legs on a narrow street, and open the door with its tinkle of welcome into a shop that will sell you eggs and sailcloth and everything in between.

MacIver knew that Dodds was a lot tougher than he looked, that he formed his own judgments on the things he cared about, that he could make sharp, accurate decisions when they were called for, and that he also maintained what he cared for with a passionate conscientiousness—the _Windrush_ was always repaired with original materials. His assumed blandness of personality in school more likely reflected on the material he was taught and on some of the teachers who taught it, than on him. He did not find them or it interesting, though he would not be obnoxious about it. In his present situation he did not care much for the high command or their grandiose strategic plans—they seemed to him to have confined the largest qualified, willing fighting force ever assembled into the most static and fatal dead-end that could be devised. What he cared for now was the thirty-man platoon that had been entrusted to him; his role, as he saw it, was to keep his men safe and their morale high; there would be no suicidal heroics, but he and his platoon would perform bravely when under grave threat. He had swiftly discerned that he had only one significant worry—Braddis.

MacIver had no questions about Dodds's power of leadership, but he did wonder why a man who cared so much about boats was not in the navy. He supposed the obverse question could be asked about him: why had someone who had spent a great many years studying the army and its behavior in World War I not pursued that interest in its sequel, but entered the navy instead? In his own case, MacIver knew there were many answers: 1) he had said some harsh things about the army, and was not sure how well he would be received there; 2) (related to above) much of what he knew about the army did not endear it to him; 3) perhaps he shared his father's distaste for "coming down in the mud." There could be many answers for Dodds, too: 1) what the navy did nowadays did not strike him as sailing at all—there was no tacking, no proper use of the wind etc.: the damn things just went where you pointed them; 2) he had already captained his own vessel, and the demotion to some humble and partial capacity, which might well not look at water at all, would certainly hurt; 3) his father, not as vague as he looked, had a parishioner who could secure a relatively quick commission for him with the Norfolks—there was nothing so promising on the navy front. MacIver thought number three was quite likely.

MacIver cooked his supper according to the Rules (tonight, humble scrambled eggs from powder, bacon, and peas) and made himself eat some of it; then he poured himself a small shot of Lagavulin and warmed it with an inch of water. The concert tonight was more Mozart, the Vespers *De Confessore;* he replayed the exquisite *Laudate dominum* three times, aching over and over at the soprano's long "Amen," the word expressing assent, and the music yearning for something more. Then he sat on sipping his scotch and retelling himself his only real war story.

Behold Lieutenant Commander MacIver on the bridge of his first and only command, the destroyer HMS *Constant,* bound from Weymouth to the French border town of Saint-Jean-de-Luz in the final fall of the war, September 1944. This made all his navy experience worthwhile—from basic training through dockyard clerk and on to the gunnery course, the post as second officer on a destroyer escorting convoys of merchant ships in the Atlantic (a post that set a high premium on staying awake), the dreary months doing secretarial duties at the Admiralty (editing the "flimsies," the annual performance ratings on every officer), and finally to promotion and this plum, thanks to a grateful admiral, who liked his writing and his rugby. "Have fun with this," Admiral Parkinson had said cheerfully. "The *Constant*'s a fine ship, though on her way to being a little dinosaur—no radar. But then your target hasn't any either, so it will be a fair match!"

Their orders were to destroy one of the last German outposts on the French Atlantic coast, and particularly the large gun emplacements on the cliffs north of the town; it had seemingly been forgotten in the withdrawal of the Wehrmacht northwards after the Normandy landing. They would land a company of the Oxfordshire and Buckinghamshire Light Infantry, under a Major Lockeford, replacing the German garrison with an Allied one. Their duties would be to maintain a border patrol and intercept enemy stragglers, especially any important ones who might be making a break southwards for neutral Spain. After landing the soldiers and giving them three days to settle themselves, they would leave, sending cordial messages from international waters to the naval commandant as they swung past San Sebastian, and head south (more greetings to Lisbon); they were to have two days at Gibraltar, and then join the Allied fleet at Toulon.

On board the *Constant* morale was high, for all the crowding from Major Lockeford's company. Leaving Weymouth at 0800 hours on a sunny morning, they had a calm uninterrupted crossing through the following night. It was warmer as they closed on the target; MacIver fancied that the offshore breezes brought them authentic scents of late summer, of the last fruits ripening, the vintage readying.

"I know this town," MacIver remarked to the major, as they sailed through the night; he had invited him to join him on the bridge. An older man, this, but footslogging solid, MacIver thought. Square face, warm brown eyes, watched your face as you talked, relaxed in response, but quicker with the leading question than to give anything away himself.

"From when?"

"1936—I was here on holiday with my girlfriend."

"You had fun?"

"We did. It was late summer, as now—wonderful fruits and vegetables, tiny sweet melons, and artichokes as big as soccer balls."

"What did you do?"

"Not a whole lot to do. We swam and ate and hiked along the cliffs and into the mountains. We watched pelota with the old men under the plane trees, and danced with the rest of the town in the square through the night after the big tuna fleet returned. Place was crawling at the time with journalists covering the Spanish civil war. Otherwise a sleepy town. Always has been, I think. Its role is to be just off to the side of the big events and personalities."

"What do you see heading in there now?"

"I see a battery of willing, ready gunners, serving under a competent officer."

He actually saw, or at least imagined, more than that. Coming down to zero hour in any competitive situation, MacIver had the habit of focusing on his opposite number, in this case the commander of the small detail left for the tail end of the Atlantic Wall. Clearly the German was no high flyer, not someone earmarked for swift promotion, but a careful, even interesting person. For your own good, you had to assume that, even at this late juncture, he and his men were still on their toes. In his mind's eye, MacIver saw a benign older man, perhaps a faded aristocrat without influence, a mere Hauptmann to whom he gave the name of Von Massenbach, a maverick teacher in a

Gymnasium, say, who still looked after his boys in this safe billet by the sea, but also taught them the discipline of gunnery, whose mathematics he had always enjoyed. He was able to translate angles and trajectories to the stretch of rock and water around them, when they still had surplus shells and could rig up decoy targets to train on. These people might have no radar directing their guns, but the schoolmaster did his best without it. MacIver could see him making practice interesting. His young battery had success with their decoy targets, and were confident they would have the same success with the real thing.

In the slack hours on the low-lit bridge, riding through the night with the quiet voices and the helmsman's silhouette off to his right, standing as easy and steady as the course, MacIver conjured up a larger context for Massenbach. He used, it seemed, unorthodox ways to keep the whole outfit alert, boredom at bay. Short rotations of actual watch, but between them games of chess (he had taught them that too), while the young hayseed from Bavaria was free to carve wood, which he did well, and the nervous painter from Darmstadt did a fresco of the medieval myth of the Venusberg at the entrance of the bunker. They spent a lot of time outside this squat pillbox, lookouts posted on cliffs for a wider survey than the slit openings the gun site provided. Keep them out in the fresh air, not stifling themselves under the low ceiling with the smell of cordite, hot steel, and oily dust. The captain himself, when he was on duty, sat in a straight-backed chair above the cliffs, facing the sea, but head bent to a book, flashing gold-rimmed glasses, trying to puzzle out the inflections of Basque grammar. Twice a week he drove into Spain in his long raking staff car to take lessons in philology from a neighboring parish priest; not for him the bored sally to Biarritz and the empty dining room of one of the old Edwardian hotels overlooking the grey Atlantic (a little more champagne, Liebchen?), keeping up pretenses for the invader. No, Massenbach was there for his men and for the town. Picnics on the beach, soccer games on the grassless field behind the lycée.

More recently though, the mood would have grown uneasy. Were they going to be marooned down here? Stern rules against the dangers of fraternization had begun to appear on the walls of their billets. In town, when the lower ranks loitered on the promenade after supper, the natives made a point of giving the cold shoulder; graffiti and tricolor stripes were found painted across the Reich's proclamations in the square; derisive shouts followed their trucks: "Hey, Bochesalop! Still hanging around, waiting to be taken? How do you think they're going to take you? Maybe from behind, eh? Storming up your ass, while you're standing at attention staring out to sea!" Massenbach's men had been schooled beyond the ordinary to tact and patience, but why were they still here?

They had taken a three-hour break after midnight, but were now back on the bridge. The question was on Major Lockeford's mind.

"Are you sure they're still here? I thought the word had gone out to the German divisions in the south that they should withdraw, and hold a line farther north."

"They were still here as of dawn yesterday morning before we left Weymouth, according to our intelligence and the local resistance. It's a puzzle: our people assume they've been left to be useful pretty much along the lines of your mission—only, I suppose, in reverse: covering the last dash of escapees across the border."

MacIver had the impression that the major had seen enough trouble in this war already, and did not relish an ill-defined and probably unnecessary engagement in this forgotten corner against the rump of the Wehrmacht. But they were getting close. An hour before dawn the men had breakfast, and then were ordered to battle stations.

Major Lockeford went back to his company. The first phase of the action would belong to the Royal Navy. The Pongoes would stay out of the way, while the *Constant*'s 4.5-inch guns eliminated the two gun sites on the cliffs. Farther inland ahead of them, the sun was already firming up with red the low clouds in the east, and starting to fire shafts of glare past the dark silhouettes of the mountains. Their targets on the coast were still in shadow but clearly visible through the glasses; the ship was now well within range, inside three miles, and turned parallel to the coast to bring forward and after guns to bear at once. This should be easy. The after guns were given the target of the more northerly placement, the forward guns the larger of the two on the cliffs to the south; they fired pretty much together, and the after guns got lucky with their first shot. MacIver on the bridge, with his glasses trained on the cliffs, felt the recoil shudder through the ship, and saw the shell explode into the rock face forming the underlip of the northern bunker, driving upwards towards the big gun itself: rock, concrete, and flame burst upwards, bright in the shadow, and a large artillery piece slid forward over the cliff. There was a cheer from soldiers and sailors on the *Constant*, but it was cut off by an answering shell from the shore, bursting not thirty yards astern. They were there after all, and they were ready.

"Two points starboard, helmsman," said MacIver, moving his glasses along the cliff to the other German gun, and seeing it flash. The forward guns had been a little high and off to the left: MacIver saw smoke rising behind the crest of the cliff.

"Two points starboard, sir," the man at the wheel repeated, making the adjustment. It wasn't enough. Instantly there was a huge explosion aft, and the whole ship lurched farther starboard, every rivet straining, as though it had just grounded itself on a rock. But it was a direct hit on the after gun turret. On the bridge they heard shouting and screams, soon drowned in the klaxon of the fire alarm blaring through the ship. They would be getting it hot and heavy now, with the enemy gun locked on their position. MacIver called for more speed, and turned the ship sharply towards the shore, heading straight for the target, offering the enemy an oncoming splinter to shoot at, which would be harder until he lined it up. The next shell from the shore fell alarmingly close on the starboard side—water from the spray struck the windows on the bridge like a detonation, and MacIver and the helmsman rocked backwards with the shock. But the next two shells in quick order fell farther back and wider from the turning ship: the German gunner had locked on their broadside course and would now have to adjust. "He damn near had me, and still might," MacIver said to himself. The forward guns blazed again below him, this time closer but low into the cliff to the right of the German battery. MacIver noticed the helmsman's mouth thin with tension as he held the wheel to the last of the turn: they both knew it was a question of who was fastest now.

"Jenkins, make your correction fast, and take the fucker out," MacIver said evenly into his intercom, and saw the officer in earphones at the forward guns glance up at the bridge and nod. "Fire and first aid parties to after gun turret." MacIver took a deep breath, and waited, trying not to count. In a matter of a few painful seconds the guns below him thundered again, and this time scored; MacIver, with his glasses locked on the bunker, willing his shells home, saw its concrete roof burst upwards and the exposed gun, no doubt with a shell in its breech, skew sideways and explode. Jenkins poured the fire on, the crews rhythmically loading four seconds to the round, and soon produced a truly pyrotechnic display across the water at the top of the cliffs, having apparently hit a magazine beside the bunker. The time was 0634. The whole engagement thus far had taken less than four minutes. It remained to be seen at what cost.

But they wouldn't stop to count it now. The engine room reported that all systems were functioning, but that it was hotter than hell down there. They asked that hoses be kept playing on the deck overhead. "Make it so, Mr. Edwards," MacIver said to his first officer, "and get me the casualty report." He addressed the ship at its battle stations: "We have taken a hit and suffered casualties, but we remain powerful, as you have seen, and will finish the job, which is to land our guests in a safe harbor. We will enter at speed, and ready to fire: the Bofors will strafe the top of the promontory heavily as we round it, so we won't have people shooting down at us. The two principal targets for the forward guns are the small pillboxes at either end of the breakwater. After that the entrance to the Hôtel de Poste, the large building at the north end of the promenade, where the enemy are billeted. I expect the action to be successfully concluded in eight to ten minutes."

In fact, it was over before 0640. The engine room gave them a burst of speed around the promontory, with the Bofors raking the high rocks; as soon as they made the turn and saw the breakwater and the town in front of them, the big guns blasted the two pillboxes. A few German soldiers suddenly appeared and started running down the breakwater towards them with machine guns chattering, as though they would stop the ship before she reached the entrance; but they were jerked like puppets off the wall by shrapnel or direct fire slamming into the stones beneath them. There was a brief pause and then the forward gun placed a 4.5-inch shell into the front door of the hotel, only half a mile away. After the explosion, figures could be seen pouring out of the ground-floor windows along with the smoke, towards trucks and jeeps in the driveway. "Wait till they're full and about to move, and fire again," MacIver said quietly into the intercom. Again the nod from Jenkins. The first round exploded the lead truck into flames, which blocked the other vehicles from the exit. A white towel attached to what looked like an officer's baton was waved from the second jeep. "Cease fire," said MacIver.

After the inferno, the silence was deafening. The engine room cut the ship's engines to idle, and she rested in the inner bay with her guns still trained on the shore, the crew at their battle stations. There were no shenanigans. Loudspeakers broadcast across the water to the German remnant that they were to pile their weapons and assemble at the north end of the promenade to await the arrival of Major Lockeford, who would receive their formal surrender. The boats were lowered and the soldiers efficiently filled them, and were powered across to the beach. They leapt ashore before the boats grounded, fanning out with weapons at the ready for the short dash up the sand. A small crowd of early-morning onlookers cheered. On the promenade, a German officer stepped forward and saluted Major Lockeford. MacIver, watching through glasses on the bridge, noted with satisfaction that he was of the rank of Hauptmann, and appeared to wear gold-rimmed glasses.

The report had been that four men had been killed and three critically injured at the after gun turret; two soldiers, who had edged too close to the action to watch the guns being worked, had been hit by shrapnel but would do fine. MacIver left the bridge in Edwards's hands, and went aft to see for himself. The gun turret was a charred husk of a thing open to the sky, its twin barrels vanished, vaporized, or exploded into myriad shrapnel fragments. What metal armament remained around the exploded core of the gun seemed frail, paper thin, a derelict black tulip; in this state, it was hard to believe the relic had ever served any kind of function at all. Spars and struts had writhed and been twisted like straws in the heat, and then set carbonized into blackness. The mechanical hoist that brought the shells up to the guns had also been seared by fire, but remained recognizable, so it was clear it had been quickly extinguished. Men from the fire party were still hosing water on the base of the turret and the surrounding deck, whose blistered paint was being stripped by the spray. MacIver congratulated the chief petty officer on their prompt reaction. "Thank you, sir," he said. "A close call—when we got here, the deck was red as a brandin' iron." The mood, MacIver noted, was somber back here, in contrast to the exultation of the forward gunners, who had not yet heard the full report.

He turned to the casualties. The two soldiers, he heard, had been helped to the sick bay, but his own men were still on the deck being attended to, on stretchers away from the heat. Four were covered with blankets and just in the process of being carried away. He stopped the first stretcher bearers, and was given the names: the body they were carrying was his junior officer Mark Cuthbertson, who had been in charge of the after gun.

Every detail of what followed was fixed in slow motion in MacIver's memory. Surgeon Lieutenant Michael Rosenberg and two of his sick-berth attendants were involved with the three other cases. When he noticed him looking down, the surgeon had given some instructions to one of the attendants, and stood up to join him. They had walked a little apart.

"So tell me, Michael," he had said.

"What we have is effectively seven fatalities. You have seen the four dead. Milnes and Oswald are unconscious and will not regain consciousness. Head wounds and burns. Matthew Barton has lost his right arm at the shoulder, and his right leg above the knee. We have stopped the bleeding there, but he also has terrible burns over more than 40 percent of the rest of his body. He can't survive." MacIver could smell burnt flesh mixed in with the lingering cordite from where they stood.

"But he's conscious?" he had said.

"Unfortunately, yes."

"What now?"

"Not long. We'll try to keep him hydrated. Apart from that, morphine and more morphine."

MacIver had gone forward and knelt beside the stretcher. "The captain's here, Matty," someone said gently.

The man had clearly registered it, and with terrible concentration tried to speak. MacIver leant forward over him to catch the slow, forced syllables, each one whispered with equal effort and emphasis. "Into the water, please, sir," he said.

"Soon, Matthew, soon," MacIver had said, afraid of his wounds but wanting to hold him.

"We will keep him comfortable, Robert," the surgeon said, when he was going back to the bridge.

"About three or four minutes of action, Michael," he said. "We lost two men a minute."

They had buried Matthew Barton at sea early in the morning on the way to Gibraltar. The two other wounded men had died within a few hours of their arrival in Saint-Jean-de-Luz, and had been buried there with the four killed at the gun turret. Matthew had slipped away into a coma, and died in the evening after they had set sail. MacIver recalled the extraordinary quiet of the ship's company, assembled for the brief service of committal. He had found it hard to read the words: "We have entrusted our brother Matthew to God's merciful keeping, and we now commit his body to the deep, in sure and certain hope of the resurrection to eternal life. . . ." The body in its weighted canvas bag covered with the Union Jack slid forward off the bier, and the light swell of the sea rose to take it, with hardly a splash. Some of his messmates had been given flowers by people in Saint-Jean-de-Luz, as part of their high-spirited thanks for liberation, and had said they would make a wreath for Matthew. MacIver now stood back and nodded to the two able seamen, who came forward with their large arrangement, beautifully woven, and lowered it evenly on new cords and laid it on the water. MacIver felt his eyes, and the whole crew's, drawn to follow it gliding away from the ship's slow passage, bobbing slightly as it passed over the small wake behind them. Then the ritual returned to the present and the words of the Navy prayer: "O Eternal Lord God, who alone spreadest out the heavens and rulest the raging of the sea; who has compassed the water with bounds until day and night come to an end: Be pleased to receive into Thy almighty and gracious protection the persons of us Thy servants and the Fleet in which we serve. Preserve us from the dangers of the sea and of the air and from the violence of the enemy; that we may be a safeguard unto our most gracious Sovereign, King George, and his dominions, and a security for such as pass upon the seas on their lawful occasions. . . ." Good strong historic words, MacIver thought as the men quietly filed away after the service, and encouraging too, as long as you live to say them. . . .

Old MacIver sat on in his rocking chair, reliving that brief passage of his life (in fact, these had been the only moments of command he had been allowed: the loss of the gun turret had necessitated a long, frustrating delay in Gibraltar for repairs, and before they were complete, it had been decided he would be more useful back in the Admiralty). But the few moments had great force for him; he could remember no others in his working life when he had felt so much alive. "You love what you do, don't you," Major Lockeford had said with a smile, but a little shake of his head as well, when they were saying good-bye, as though he had been doing nothing but this sort of thing through the whole war. MacIver only came to realize later that the shake of the head implied a small criticism from a generous man, or at least an incomprehension: how can you radiate such exultation at the outcome, when you have just lost seven men whom you obviously cared about? His best friend at Oxford, the little fire-plug of a scrum-half for the university, Terry Aldington, had once told him in a moment of truth: "The thing about you is that you have a lot of violence in your nature, and only a piece of you disapproves of the fact: you had better find a gentle girl and marry her, so you can learn the rest." Terry, who had been killed in the Normandy landings, was never wrong, and MacIver did what he was told. The question, though, was always how well he had learned the lessons she had taught him.

CHAPTER 5

The Art of Seeing Differently

Not a good night, but still bearable. Pain a little more assertive, fever spiking higher, before the dawn remission, sinking with the moon. Pain and fear both know that a little goes a long way at night. They had been testing him. But he now had to acknowledge that he was persistently ill, in a particularly nagging way. The pain seemed to have opened up a second front with some sudden thrusts into his midsection while he was writing—as though it weren't hard enough already. But perhaps the most telling symptom was that he was now finding it very hard to swallow—the only thing attracting appetite was the warm water. He still tried to abide by the Rules and eat real food, but he was aware he pushed it around inside his mouth, gumming it like a child who has been told to finish her spinach or rice pudding if she wants to watch her favorite program, which is just about to start. Tears would not be far away. In his case, it was not so much revulsion at the taste, but fear of the stab at the act of swallowing.

However, at this stage no one was going to push him around. There were rules he was prepared to trample, and food rules were some of them; they were his damn rules after all. *L'état c'est moi,* said Louis XIV, and Cromwell had said it better the year before to the Rump Parliament: "Ye have sat too long for any good ye have done, in the name of God now go"—as fine a run of monosyllables (all but one word!) as there is in the English language. Burke could not have written that sentence. When you start a century with Shakespeare, you definitely have a leg up on strong language. After that, decay into forced rhythm and flatulence, or as the Greeks called it, "frigidity." Enough!

Anyway, he was not condoning, let alone advocating, anarchy; he was just bending the rule on food. He knew he had to make himself eat, but he was taking a one-day furlough. Today it would be water, tomorrow he would eat what he could swallow. But meanwhile he was wasting time. He needed to get to work. And in fact, here he should pick up his pace while he could, because the signs were he would not be able to go on a whole lot longer. He needed another character, but he had time for only one more. It would be Tim Callum, the artist whose sketch Braddis had trashed.

Private Tim Callum
ARTIST

Tim Callum, born January 6, 1899, oldest son of Yarmouth fisherman, aspiring, basically untaught painter. Drafted into Norfolks, March 1, 1917. Mother had died when he was ten. Father dour, silent, decent, had struggled hard for the four children. Dour silence passed from father to son, but from the earliest age a crayon in the hand, and an ease in making any shape—shading, perspective, point of view, human figure, animals, landscape, seascape—came to him quite naturally. He could copy anything, and in doing it he could see what the artist had intended and what skills or tricks he had used to get there. The hint of larger dimensions came through for him from an elderly spinster teacher at the local school, Miss Ann Houghton, the year after his mother died. She had marched him off in virtual silence to the public library, where she was clearly a respected figure; she went up to the desk and was handed two books they had been holding for her. She took him over to a table, and opened both books to particular pages: "Here," she said finally, "look at these. This one is a painting by an American, Fitz Hugh Lane, of a place called Brace's Rock on the Atlantic coast of Massachusetts. He painted the same scene at least three times in 1864. He was paralyzed in the legs as a boy and often had to be propped up in a boat to paint the sea scenes that he loved. This one is by our own Turner, perhaps our greatest painter; it's called *Wreck Buoy,* and he first painted it in about 1807 and came back to it forty years later. Pretty much the same Atlantic water. Do you like them?"

"Yes, I like them both a lot."

"I knew you would; we both like them a lot. But do they look like any sea you or your father has seen?"

"Not really. This one may be too rough, and the other too flat."

"Do they look like anything the painters had seen?"

"Maybe something they had seen with a special eye, not an everyday eye."

"Exactly so. You're an artist, not just a painter. An artist is someone who makes us see things we wouldn't otherwise have seen for ourselves. You're getting old enough not just to copy other painters' pictures, but to paint your own."

The next year he had done a pencil drawing of his father at home after the day's haul, staring into the fire. It was basically a picture of weariness in the bone, one arm hooked and hanging over the top of the cane chair, collarless shirt open and hanging over the pants, neck muscles stringy and corded around the clavicle, boots on the hearth and socked feet extended, eyes flat and staring unseeing into the flames. He took it to school and showed it to Miss Houghton, though she was no longer teaching him; he waited outside her classroom and took it in to her at the end of the day, putting it on the desk without a word. She looked at it a long time, and eventually said, "It's a wonderful drawing, Tim; it's everything I hoped of you."

"Do you think it's grim?"

"I think it's sad," she said.

"I think everything I paint or draw for myself will be hard and grim," he said, correcting her without emphasis.

"I think it will be for a while," she said and handed the picture back to him. It's not just that the boy has grey seawater in his veins, she thought; he has a whole freezing, featureless ocean of it, and he must find a way to let it out.

Miss Houghton had seen, and could see, a lot, but never anything like this, he often thought, looking out over the desolation of the Ypres salient beyond the Norfolks' trench. Still, it was not so bad. His father had quietly approved his decision: "Fair enough," he had said. "Go and do your bit." Tim had been able to send some money home from his pittance of a pay packet each month—more useful to his dad than the time he had spent watching his younger brother and sisters. He could live here all right. He needed nothing but sketchbook and pencil, and a little set aside in case he got a bit of leave and a chance to go somewhere and paint. In the meantime he was learning things; he had learnt to admire Lieutenant Dodds and to hate Sergeant Braddis.

．　．　．

MacIver now had the players he needed to mount his last movement. He went off to mouth some more toast, and varied the honey and tea with some hot chocolate, dunking the one in the other. Then more of the Oldies and Goodies, music and the single malt. Tonight they played Beethoven's Archduke Trio, Ax-Kim-Ma. "Seven letters encompassing a trinity of musical perfection," he announced to the room, as though he were their agent introducing them from the stage. Four movements, not a clunker among them, but the one he would follow closest was the slow one, another instance of hesitancy growing to assertiveness. In this case, the assertiveness came, MacIver believed, from an unusually frequent use of repetition, the same note struck again and again in each stage of the progression of the theme, at first tentatively but building to the point of relentlessness, especially in the piano. The piece is close to the high mark of Beethoven's best, but MacIver thought it might also be an indication of his growing deafness. When they came to the composer's rooms after his death, they found amid the general mess that the strings in his piano had been broken and sprung in tangles above the frame, from his repeated hammering on the keys, again and again, to make him hear himself. Might this not be a case where the involuntary mannerism of frustration had been transformed into the device of a musical and moving insistence?

MacIver went to bed, cautiously, and lay there remembering the first time he met his wife, Margaret, that recurrent and time-worn refrain of the war-torn. He met her first at the Gordon Gallery on Fifty-seventh Street, in the fall of 1947, his second year as a professor at Columbia after his release from the navy. In a literal sense, he had been in the wrong place at the wrong time. A friend had told him about an exhibition of World War I photographs in midtown. There were meant to be some hitherto unknown amateur ones by soldiers serving in the trenches; one of them was said to be a "Wilfred Owen with a camera." The trouble was the show was over, and it had not been at the Gordon Gallery, as MacIver had been told, but at the Goreham Gallery two blocks farther east.

MacIver had gone first to the Gordon Gallery at twelve-thirty on a Saturday afternoon, and it had been still closed, but due to open at one o'clock. The sign outside had said nothing about photographs; it advertised new paintings by Margaret Westleigh. Looking through the glass door, he could see the paintings on the wall to the right, but sitting on the sofa with her back to them was a high-breasted young woman with a lot of rich brown hair cascading in waves over her shoulders. She was looking up and a little to the right and seemed to be studying another painting on the wall in front of her, which he could not see. But her absorption left him free to study her unobserved. To this day, if he were a painter himself, he could make a completely accurate representation of her as he saw her then. Her legs were crossed, and the light along the line of her raised chin was reproduced exactly on the three and a half inches of trim left ankle showing below the long, flared skirt. One black leather pump dangled off her toes, the heel pointing at the floor. Perhaps he moved and caught her eye, or else the force of his scrutiny pulled her attention to him, but after what he thought must have been several minutes, she turned and saw him. He could not tell if she was aware of his watching her for so long, but if so, she showed no irritation or surprise. She took his presence in with the same calm consideration she was giving the picture, and instead of waving him away, stood up and moved gracefully to the door.

"World War One photos?" he had asked.

"Photos?" she had repeated. "Not here." A pause before she remembered. "Ah, yes, I think you want the Goreham show, a couple of blocks down on the right. But haven't they finished?"

"Quite possibly they have. All my information seems wrong so far. I was told they were here. If they're still at the Goreham, would they be closed too? I thought they opened at noon."

"Yes, I think you might be right there. We don't open till one."

"Well, I had better go and check them out," he said a little lamely. "These seem interesting," he added, nodding towards the paintings on the far wall.

"I hope so," she said, with only the trace of a smile.

He had thanked her, and dutifully gone down to the Goreham. She was right: no more World War I photos, he was a week late. They had moved on to a gallery in Washington. Maybe he could pursue them there? Very possibly, he had said. At the moment he found himself more interested in the show at the Gordon. But first he would get a beer.

The door to the Gordon Gallery was open when he returned, and the young woman still had the place to herself. She was busying herself at the desk in the alcove, and looked up when he entered. Try as he might, then and later, he could not read anything into her pleasant greeting.

"No World War One?" she asked.

"No, apparently it's started a new campaign in Washington. But I thought I would come back here and look at these paintings a little closer up."

"The Goreham's loss is our gain," she said, but not flirting; she was already back among her papers. There was nothing for it but to look at the paintings.

He thought that the paintings, now that he attended to them properly, were very fine. They walked a slightly discomforting line between the inside and outside worlds. The viewer was always outside, looking into a room, or some kind of inhabited space. There was sometimes a stone wall or mullioned window alongside him, on two or three even a climbing rose or creeper, but the view of the picture was always into an interior, where, however, the light was never directed for the viewer's benefit. There were shadowy figures, sometimes, in the inside space, not necessarily in the background, but the band of light looked past them, just as it did past the photograph or small figurine or bowl of flowers on the table against the wall. The effect on the viewer was of being excluded from a life being lived; when he later read the blurbs on the brochure, he found that a distinguished critic had said that "the paintings are of deeply haunted spaces, where figures and objects have their own full sense of belonging, which the viewer, however intently he looks, can never completely enter: we are always being tactfully reminded that, in any complete sense, we are outside 'true' history. . . ."

MacIver went to the desk and asked for a price list, and some information about the artist. The young woman handed him the two brochures with a smile. There was one recent small painting entitled *James Merrill's Birdcage and Ms.* The shadow of a bird in its cage fell across the open page of the book, on which verses, phrases, and half lines were written in the young poet's beautiful handwriting at apparently haphazard angles to one another. The composition of the whole page made a kind of mosaic of poetry. Surprisingly, MacIver knew the photograph from which the painting had been made. He had given a talk at a university in the early spring on oral history and its limitations; James Merrill, maybe still an undergraduate, had attended the talk and come up to speak to him afterwards, and followed it up, with his lovely courtesy, by sending the photograph he had taken, a set of variations on the theme of the fleeting held captive. What had struck him was MacIver's insistence in the course of his talk that we must not assume that oral history ever gives us the whole history, "any more than the ornithologist, who records a snatch of birdsong, has caught the bird."

The painter had honored the theme, but not in any slavish way. The translation from black and white to color had allowed the artist to play further with textures. The light from the open window was filtered through a fold of lace curtain, whose swaying shadow played with the others on the book and the table. It was a lovely, devoted piece of work; and looking for the ominous red dot on the price list, he saw that it was still available and that he could just afford it. He was very excited about it, and turned for the first time to the brochure to find out more about the artist. Before he could start reading about her, he was pulled up short by another photograph on the front page: the young woman behind the desk was Margaret Westleigh. He got past the first irrational flicker of indignation (had he not been duped in some way?), and read on for the conventional facts (Slade School of Art in Oxford; exhibitions in London, Edinburgh, Zurich, New York, Santa Fe, etc.; works bought by National Portrait Gallery, London; the Fitzwilliam Museum, Cambridge; Harvard University . . .). Plenty of discriminating buyers, but not many large corporate ones; her works may have been too intimate and on too small a scale for the boardroom. Their loss! Well, now he would be a discriminating buyer himself.

He went to the desk, and said, trying to keep the note of accusation out of his voice, "You're Margaret Westleigh."

"Yes."

He nodded. "I would like to buy number fifteen, if it's still available. I have the photograph, and I'd like to mate it with the painting. I think it's an extremely loving and imaginative extension of it. How did you get it, by the way?"

"My parents have a house next to his parents in the south of France. We were both visiting at the same time, and we met there. He seemed to me the most remarkable man, and scarily bright. Afterwards, he sent me a postcard of the photo with a reference to something he thought I would enjoy. I forgot the reference, but I loved the picture and thought I would do this small painting of it in his honor. And you, how did you get yours?"

MacIver explained, and went on: "But it's a private thing. Perhaps you want to keep it."

"No," she laughed. "I just want to keep the postcard. But I'm glad you like the painting so much."

"I'm delighted with it," he said. "Do you own this gallery, too?"

"Good heavens, no! It's Sally Gordon's. Her assistant is getting married today, and Sally's at the wedding, so I said I would mind the store. I wanted to take a fresh look at some of these pictures hanging here in neutral space; I'm considering letting in more light on my next crop."

He was shocked. "Why change anything?" he said, instantly regretting the heavy note of Caledonian gallantry.

She was amused at his fervor, but he was looking at her very straight.

"My name is Robert MacIver," he said, handing her his check. "Would you allow me to celebrate this big event for me, by having dinner with me tonight?" His eyes never left her face, and the truth was she had no plans.

He had taken her to Arcadia, and they had had a wonderful evening.

CHAPTER 6

Trophies

Like an enemy that has bombed its weaker opponent close to final submission, MacIver's illness could now dispense with any distinction between daytime and nighttime activities: there would be insignificant resistance at whatever hour it struck. He had felt awful when he woke up, the fever not ebbing one jot at dawn; he had become light-headed in the shower stall, and after apparently bouncing off the walls on his way down, he had found himself on all fours on the floor, with the water obliviously pounding him from above. It seemed unsafe to try and stand up in this confined space, but he had managed to butt the door of the shower open with his head, and then crawl out onto the bath mat. He had pulled towels off the racks to dry himself and keep warm, and, feeling a little better, he had crawled to the toilet and managed to climb up and sit on it. Finally, his head seeming steadier now, he had stood up, returned to the shower stall, turned off the water, and closed the door. He judged his performance during this episode undignified, and probably comical to any observer, but in the circumstances resourceful. He felt he had, over about the same time period, recapitulated the essential progression of evolution: the aquatic animal coming onto dry land, then achieving four-legged locomotion, and finally standing as *Homo erectus* on two legs. Impressive. For breakfast he had bread and Tawny marmalade, pausing with each mouthful, allowing himself to relish the taste of the Tawny, and then sipping the warm water and preparing to pay the cost of the swallow. By the end, he felt he had defeated heavy odds and was ready for work. Today he intended to bring Simon Dodds and Tim Callum together.

Lieutenant Dodds had asked Private Callum to come and see him in what passed for his office in the company headquarters. It was his habit to spend more time in the trench with his platoon than most officers found necessary, and on one occasion he had noticed Callum sketching, after he had been relieved from his watch on the fire-step. Dodds had asked politely if he could see the book, and Callum had passed it over, he thought, resignedly, as though this would mean more trouble. The drawings struck Dodds as very powerful—some of men sleeping, men cleaning their kit, men horsing around on their weekly visit to the bathhouse, and one ferocious cartoon of Sergeant Braddis apparently playing with his bayonet. The quality of the work seemed so obvious to him—but what did he know?—that he wanted to encourage Callum. He had heard that the Artists' Rifles, a pretty wild bunch by all accounts, whose sector of the trench system was less than four hundred yards from theirs, held what they called soirées at a local estaminet behind the lines, at which there was a lot of bad wine, some poetry reading, some holding forth, but also some sharing of thoughts on work they were doing or planning. An arty officer of the group had told Dodds of these occasions, giving time and place, when he had mentioned Callum, and conveyed that he would be entirely welcome ("God in heaven," he had actually said, "half of them are so far gone, they couldn't recognize their own platoon mates"). "You should go," Dodds said, "and take that book with you. I hear they occasionally have famous artists, or at least Official War Artists, soaking up the atmosphere, and spreading their wide culture for the rest of us poor fellows, for our morale."

"I don't know if that's my sort of thing, sir," said Callum. "I do best as a sort of loner."

"That's probably so," said Dodds easily. He had one leg up on his desk, and was idly letting an antique gold watch swing from its chain around his finger. "But a change of scene does us all good from time to time, even if it makes us say, 'This is definitely not my scene.' "

"That may be true." He was noticing the swaying watch dart its Tinker Bell dance off the walls. "That looks a lovely old watch, sir."

"Yes. It's more than a hundred years old—made by Robert Pennington of London about 1810, I think." And he decided to tell him the story. "It's the only trophy I ever won, and it's the one I wanted most. It's a Norfolk story, so a Norfolk lad will get the point of it. We lived on the Broads, and as long as I can remember, I loved sailing. My grandfather, Augustus Dodds, who lived up the river from us (*smack* on the river: when it was running dangerously high, he could dangle his feet in the water from his porch)—he gave me this nice little dinghy, which I sailed everywhere, morning, noon, and night. So when I was about fifteen, he asked me to come to tea, as he sometimes did, and to arrive at 4:15 prompt. If I made it on time, he would give me this watch. Now he knew that the tide turned at 3:40 on that day, and when the tide turns down with the current on the Bure, it's carrying a weight of water, and no little dinghy is going to make its way up against it. So my trip on that afternoon, which with the tide I could do in half an hour, would take forever. So my grandfather was testing me to see if I knew my tides. Oh, yes—and this is important—he also made the condition that I could not leave my house before 3:30, and said he would check with my mother to make sure I hadn't cheated. I knew my tides, and there was no chance, coming straight upstream on the Bure at 3:30 that afternoon, I could make it by 4:15. But I also knew that after the tide turns, the Bure, by a quirk of current, flushes some of its water all the way up a cutting near our house, to re-join the main stream on one of its crazy bends three quarters of a mile *above* my grandfather's house. A truly circular flow. I also knew that cutting had been dredged recently, so I wouldn't get stuck. It would take me a quarter of an hour to work my way up the cut, but that left me plenty of time to come racing down the Bure in time for tea, tying the painter at 4:11. My grandfather was sitting on the porch lazily swinging the watch—as I notice I have been doing."

"Does that mean I get the watch now, for coming on time?" said Callum.

"Afraid not, my lad," said Dodds, laughing and surprised.

"Do you think your grandfather knew about the cutting?"

"I wondered about that at the time, or whether I pulled a fast one on him. But now I'm sure he knew, and wanted me to have the satisfaction of outsmarting him. After all, he was sitting there before I got there, and I got there by the only way there was. I think he just wanted to give me the watch."

"A generous man."

"Yes. I think about him often, checking the time for this or that, on this lovely old watch. The landscapes, here and there, were meant to be similar, flat, well-watered, under big skies, but look what we've done with this. And the watch was meant to be there to time the drift of sky and water, and here it is still ticking away in a filthy time and place. But thanks for listening to my story."

"I liked it," said Callum. "You were a kind of Odysseus, weren't you, making all your voyages and knowing all the ins and outs on the Broads? The *Odyssey* was the only book I ever got to love in school. But that watch, sir, that's a great prize, and you won it fair and true."

"How do you get on with Sergeant Braddis?" Dodds asked casually, as he was taking him to the door.

"He's a weird cuss, but I don't let him get to me."

"Right attitude. Well, good-bye, and think about giving the Artists a chance."

"I will, sir," said Callum.

Dodds was impressed with Callum—watchful, wary, but entirely his own man, he thought. He wondered if he would make it to the Artists' party. Perhaps he was too independent to need other people's good opinion of his work; if you'd come this far alone, why bother to attend to what was going on in other sketchbooks. Still, wouldn't you, even if entirely secure in your own sense of direction, be at least *curious* where others were heading, even as you struck out on your own? But never mind Callum. Dodds was more concerned with Braddis. He had heard of the destruction of Callum's sketch, and had been told that the sergeant had also confiscated another one, supposedly a nude. This was unacceptable behavior, making life miserable for a particular member of the platoon—so blatant that everyone had noticed it. Dodds had also heard of Braddis's solo expeditions into no-man's-land in the small hours. He thought there could only be one reason behind those, but to check his hunch, he would have to go to town himself.

. . .

Supper: scrambled eggs and warm water. Music: Schubert's Cello Quintet. He and Margaret had attended a performance of the piece by the Guarneri, plus Rostropovich, at Queen Elizabeth Hall in London just after Benjamin Britten had died, in the spring of 1977. Britten had asked that they play the slow movement of it at his memorial service in Westminster Abbey— a nice instance of the public concert being a warm-up for the smaller audience. Listening to it then and now, it was clear why the composer wanted it: he would have liked the clean deliberation of the movement (literally *picked* clean, with all that pizzicato) advancing slowly to its gently measured, thoughtful conclusions, but suddenly swept away by the wonderfully agitated churning, a whirr of strings protesting that passion should never be so subdued. It happens twice, but measure reigns again at the end.

MacIver sat listening with his Lagavulin in his paw, in the fire's glow with the last of the loose planks he'd managed to gather, without tumbling down the chute again, from the ruined porch. Alas, if the cold held up, it would soon come to book burning. Neither the whisky nor the fire could quell his shivers. But he sat on after the music, thinking as he liked to do, about his boyhood on Loch Affric.

He did not have to close his eyes to be able to summon up the whitewashed stone house standing on its narrow lawn facing the lake, and the small boathouse off to the left. How many times had he rowed his dinghy on a breathlessly calm day across the house's reflection in the lake, sometimes so clear that he believed he could detect, staring down on it, where the black paint trim was chipped or peeling; he imagined he could count the hairs around each claw on the brass lion's foot, the massive doorknob set in the middle of the front door, and trace the figure in the oak around it. The water was pure and healthy at that time, but with a brownish tint from the bottom, which the trout hovering/browsing/nosing up under the banks shared, and perhaps a small hint of peat in the taste, like a good single malt.

Sometimes after school the boy could persuade his mother to let him take her for a row on the lake; at nine or ten, he found the boat still a little wide for him, but he would pull mightily, taking pride in the blisters, as he looped the oars in a big arc out of the lake and around and back into it, high enough to allow water to trickle down from the blades and off the handles and form a little puddle around his stout shoes. "Rest a little," his mother would say, when they had reached the middle of the narrow lake. He would rest on his oars, and take in the steep russet hills rising around them, the house looking gravely across at them from afternoon shadow.

The quiet of these scenes, with the smallest lapping of water against the hull, sank deep into him, and he returned to them often. His mother in color and mood was always integral to them; he could see her in skirt and sweater, leaning back on the cushions with her legs tucked under her, a slender figure with wisps of auburn hair around her face, trailing her hand abstractedly in the water, rocking slightly forward each time the blade caught, always cool and serene, but usually, he later realized, somewhere else. Sometimes they would pause for a quarter hour or more, watching birds flying off the water and in the sky overhead, MacIver always sweeping the sky intently, always hoping to show her the great golden eagle whose nest he knew on a crag high above the house. Occasionally his mother would become part of it, pointing out tricks of light on the water, cat's-paws chasing into the shallows with the first breath of evening wind.

Then they would head back, and it would be a point of pride with him that he could, by plotting his position against the opposite shore, navigate himself straight into the dark of the boathouse without having to turn around. But he let his mother help him. "A little more left hand," she would say quietly at the critical juncture, and he would steal a glimpse of the corner of the dock as he made the adjustment. Then he would ship his oars and they would glide to rest in the little boat's berth; he would tie the painter to the ring, gallantly hand his mother ashore, and carry his oars across his skinny shoulders up to the lonely house. Home is the sailor, home from the sea.

MacIver realized he seemed to be making some kind of tally of his memories, as though completing the inventory might tell him what his life amounted to. But why not? It was implausible that the account should be held open for future contributions. So let it rip! The lake and the eagle led him ineluctably on to the most astonishing and terrifying encounter of all—the story of the eagle's egg. It had been a large temptation ever since the boys had observed that the big gold-ruffed bird had a mate keeping him company on the nest.

So in the middle of April when he was ten, Robert MacIver, urged on by his friends and schoolmates Hamish Morrison and another Robert, Bobby Nairn, decided to take an egg, in the temporary absence of its parents, from the nest at the top of the cliff above the loch. The nest was in a small stunted pine that jutted out over the cliff from a fissure in the granite. He reached in from below and took the nearer of two eggs. It was at least three and a half inches long, and quite wide too, and the texture of the shell to his first unseeing touch was distinctly rough. It weighed in his hand and felt warm as he cupped it carefully, scrabbling down the stunted pine tree using one arm and his legs for grip, and skinning the inside of his thighs in the descent; they had all come straight from school and were wearing their uniform grey flannel shorts.

Once down on the rocky ledge under the pine, he examined his trophy carefully; it was strongly marked with buff and ruddy brown dashes and streaks, and rounder—less pointed—than the woodcock's and curlew's eggs in his collection, though not as round as the pheasant's. He was breathless from his nervous climb, and also in terror of the lurking fierce eye, hooked talons and beak, and giant wingspan from which he'd stolen it; he understood the same qualities were somewhere there, confined inside the shell in his soft hands. The other boys had gathered close, a knot of three tousled heads staring at the prize. He let them both hold it briefly, and they were reverent to it too. "The biggest and best we've ever touched," declared Hamish. But he and Bobby both understood that the egg was Robert's.

But in the night things changed. He would have to take it back. His need to do so grew with the hours. He could not sleep, his bed not snug now against the wind off the lake, storming the pines to east and west of the house, the rain squalls drumming into the windowpanes. Lying there, he stared at the window, trying to see past the leaded mullions to the outside, but the dark was giving no quarter tonight, advancing right to the frame, black on deeper black. The trouble was the egg itself, which he had nested in a bowl shaped from his best sweaters in the second drawer. He had left the drawer open about four inches, so there could be some circulation of air around it. But in the night he had started having serious doubts whether this was enough. Maybe the power of the bird, curled inside its oatmealy shell—all that steely wildness driving to grow and be unleashed, maybe it needed to feel the great dome of sky overhead to endure its rounded confinement till it was ready. It was the egg that was haunting him. Maybe he was stifling it there in the drawer; he could feel it raging at him from among the sweaters, and despising him: what did he know about nursing anything this big and wild?

He would take it back first thing in the morning. It was a Saturday, not a school day, so his mother would sleep late. He knew from her minimal signs of disapproval (a shake of the head, a thinner line to the mouth, once a "Couldn't you leave it for them?") at his previous trophies that he should not show her this one. This one was different, bigger and crueler, and taunting him with a taboo: he shuddered to think what would happen to him if he bored his holes at each end and blew it clean for his egg collection.

Up before six, and out the back door, and up the track through the woods behind the house; the wind, tamer by dawn, was still gusting through the pines, spraying the stored rain on his head and sweater—the air as fresh and cold between his fingers as water from the burn. Up the sodden path, his gym shoes soaked (he had thought they would give him better purchase than the boots when he climbed the tree this time), carrying the egg in his right hand wrapped in a clean handkerchief; he didn't want it smelling of him when it was back in the nest. Higher now above the lake, and brighter now as the trees thinned, grey clouds scudding fast and furious across the palest blue, quite a bit of silver behind him at the end of the lake, where the sun was massing for a breakthrough.

He came out onto the flat bare terrace of rock above the cliff. Some of the stones held puddles of water from the night's storm. Over the lip of the cliff, the pine tree jutted, some of the rugged nest of twigs visible. But he couldn't see if the birds were there. He put the egg down gently, still wrapped in its handkerchief, in a little hollow, and crossed the clearing to where there was a tall rock that would give him a better view. The nest seemed to be empty; clearly eagles started their sky patrol early. There was no point in his hanging around. He retrieved the egg, went straight to the tree, and began his climb again out over the overhang. It seemed harder today without his friends to encourage him and impress, and the red, flaky bark was now pulpy wet and slippery after the rain. Yesterday's grazes were still tender under his overalls.

It took longer, but he finally climbed as high as yesterday's mark, from which he could reach into the nest and leave the egg. He turned it in his hand so he could put it down in the nest and take the handkerchief away without jolting or dropping it. He reached in exactly as he had yesterday, and at that moment an eagle, with a terrifying scream, soared up at him from below the cliff edge, vast wingspan, wider than his father was tall, raised high and back, and talons extended.

Robert froze, his hand still extended into the nest, his head involuntarily tucked down hard against his arm. The bird sailed across the nest and Robert felt a searing-hot pain across the back of his hand and scalp, as the stretched talons scored a groove and passed over. Blood started coming down into his eyes, but he wasn't yet aware of it. The shock of that looming fury from below the lip of the gorge galvanized him. He slid down the tree like a chute and scrambled tripping across the clearing, his only preoccupation being to get under the cover of the woods before the bird returned for its second run. If he was still in the open, he knew it would kill him; the only thing that had saved him so far was his clinging to the protection of the tree, which was hard for such a large bird to negotiate. He just made it back to the woods. He heard another fierce scream, and the flutter of powerful wings overhead, as he rolled tight as a hedgehog between a rock and the base of a pine.

He had scant memory of his stumbling descent through the woods. Apparently, he had pulled his sweater up over his head to stop the blood flowing into his eyes. His mother must have needed all her cool temperament to handle the sight of the gory little ghoul who had staggered through the kitchen door. He managed to say with some insistence that he was putting the egg back, as though the bird was being unreasonable. But his mother straightened that out: "Putting the egg back was the right thing; what he was punishing you for was your taking it yesterday. I never intervene in your woodland adventures, but right now I'm putting a two-month ban on all bird nesting. And don't think your father will lift it when he comes back." She had managed to repair the gash in the back of his hand. "But I don't think I should do your head wound. I can't really see how bad it is through all the hair. I'm afraid we'll have to go to Dr. Macleod's surgery." Which was no fun. The doctor shaved his head along the line of the talon's gouge, and poured liberal amounts of iodine into the wound for cleansing, before closing the deepest part of it with four stitches. He did not yell, but the tears rolled down his face. "Cheer up, young Robert," said the doctor, going about his work. "It's not everyone who's been scored by an eagle." And indeed, he found that his wound, and the way he had got it, earned him considerable cachet in the playground. At recess his classmates would line up for the ritual bowing of his head.

CHAPTER 7

The Last Pulse of Reverie

Another poor night; there was no dramatic bolt of pain, but the screws of the fever were being turned tighter on him all around, he felt, and whatever tissues within were being racked, they were now, he imagined, paper thin and would soon tear away. He did not have what Margaret had had, but, whatever it was, it clearly had the strength to do the same job. And wasn't that what he wanted?

He tried soup for breakfast, turning the day upside down, but knowing he could not chew. Then painfully but eagerly he went to work:

Sergeant Braddis had come smartly to attention and saluted in front of his young superior, Lieutenant Dodds, his great dagger thumbnails in evidence at the front of his loosely closed fists. Dodds, seated, neat in his uniform, looked up at him appraisingly. The man, on the surface, was every inch a soldier—a billboard for the regular army. "At ease, Sergeant," he said, easily, and proceeded to the point; to beat about the bush with such a man would be to lose the skirmish before you started. "I want to question you about two points of your behavior which are troubling to me, and to hear your answers on them."

"Certainly, sir. I'm sorry if I've dissatisfied you." Not a sign of discomfort there, Dodds saw; perhaps his best chance of getting anywhere would come from Braddis underestimating him.

"My first point concerns Private Callum."

"Sir?"

"There is a perception in the platoon that you pick on him."

"For what, sir?"

"I understand you destroyed a sketch he was making during his stand-down time in the trench."

"Yes, sir, that was a mistake on my part, and I apologized for it. I was cleaning my bayonet, and he was drawing something, and kept looking at me furtive-like, and it looked to me as though he was doing a cartoon of me, which he could show around when I wasn't there, and make me a laughingstock. A kind of sneaky insubordination, if you see what I mean, sir. So I swooped down and tore it up. Then he said he wasn't drawing me, so I apologized."

"There was another drawing that you confiscated from him, of a nude, a naked woman."

"Yes, sir. That was different. He had this picture, very lifelike, I have to hand it to him, of a woman standing in a bathtub full frontal showing everything she had. I considered it a lewd picture. Then there are others I have seen he's drawn of the men, without their permission, naked at the baths. Now I know you're fond of the lad, sir, and he may well be good at drawing and other things, but it seems to me that he's not a soldier. Here we are facing a well-armed and well-trained enemy less than three hundred yards away in a very difficult war, and he's sitting by himself painting naked men and ladies. He's never part of the platoon, just sits there doodling. So I took away the picture as a signal to him that I wanted him to shape up. Otherwise, he's just one more thing I have to worry about when we go over the top—and as you should know, sir, Mr. Jerry requires all our attention."

"Where is the picture now, Braddis?"

"I have it in the sergeants' mess, sir."

"I want you to give it back to him. You can say you asked me about it, and I said it was all right for him to draw what he likes, as long as he takes care of his soldierly work."

"I don't think I want to do that, sir. That way I lose face in the platoon."

"All right. Then bring it to me this afternoon, and I'll give it back to him. I'll tell him you brought it to me for my decision."

"All right, sir. That way would be a little better."

"Good. This afternoon, then. The other point is this: you must stop your solo patrols into no-man's-land at night." Dodds was watching the sergeant closely. Perhaps a small clenching of the jaw, but perhaps he was imagining it.

"And why is that, sir? I'm off duty after the regular patrol, so isn't my time my own?"

"Yes, but not if you're endangering yourself: we have enough casualties in regular encounters without losing sergeants on personal sprees."

"They're not sprees, sir, and I do know how to look after myself."

"There is the additional reason that you make these patrols for dishonorable purposes."

"And what would they be? Killing Germans?"

Better, thought Dodds. He's getting angry.

"Looting, Sergeant."

"Understand me here, sir," said Braddis, with heavy emphasis on the *sir*. "I am a good professional soldier; there are not that many of us—maybe just enough to have kept England in the war, amid a bunch of amateurs sitting on their duffs and waiting for victory to be delivered to them without getting dirty. I don't believe we would be widely blamed if, after removing one of the king's enemies, we took away with us some small token of our victory."

"That might be so, if the tokens came only from the enemy. But the feeling would be very different if it was known that some of them came from our own good men, fallen for the same king—even if the tokens were taken by our professional soldiers."

"I can assure you, sir, that the few things I have taken have come from fallen enemy."

"Well, let's see now," said Dodds. He reached into the drawer of his desk, and took out a hip flask of heavy decorated silver and put it on the desk. He certainly had Braddis's attention now. "I am told that this is nineteenth-century Bavarian silver, so we can assume it came from a German source. But this"—he reached into the drawer again, came up with a slim silver cigarette case, and placed it on the desk next to the flask—"belonged to my friend Lieutenant Kenneth Thomas of the Royal Welsh Fusiliers, who was reported 'missing in action, presumed dead,' not half a mile from where I'm sitting, after an unsuccessful sally seven weeks ago. It actually has his monogram *KLT* engraved on the front, and I happen to know that it was a present to him from his young wife."

There was no bluster in the man now. He was not rattled, but he was concentrating. Dodds's eyes never left his face, and he saw a great stillness come into his expression. This was war, and Braddis was not underestimating him now.

"May I ask where you got these things, sir?" he said quietly.

"You may. I got them from the same man you sold them to, Frédéric Cafors, the pawnbroker on the Rue de Beauvais in Amiens."

"How do you—or he—know I was the one who sold them to him? Twenty people a day take their swag to Cafors."

"So you do know the establishment. And it's true—he runs a busy business; and sometimes more than one person is there at once. You had been identified by someone as a sergeant of the Norfolks (he pronounced our regiment as though it was German), and frankly, Sergeant, your finger- and thumbnails are quite distinctive marks of identity."

There was no doubt about it: the soft-looking little shit was tougher than Braddis thought.

"What do you intend to do with these things, sir?" he asked.

"I intend to send the cigarette case back home, where it belongs, to Mr. Thomas's widow," Dodds said. "But right now I want to add something else. You are, as you say, a very good professional soldier, and we need them badly. But there is something in your temperament which seems to tempt you out of bounds; I am aware of the incident at Caterham at the guards' depot, when you were a strong candidate for the next plum regimental sergeant major's position that came up." (For God's sake, it was in the man's file: he had been busted to sergeant for purloining stores when he was quartermaster at the depot.) "I think you should stay within bounds and within rules, and you will be all right."

"Will that be all, sir?"

"Yes. And remember the picture by this afternoon."

"Sir." He had saluted smartly and marched away, himself a picture of contained rage; but Callum's drawing had duly been dropped off at the office in a brown envelope, boldly addressed: ATTENTION: LIEUT. DODDS. The picture was quite unmarked, slightly to his surprise, and Dodds found it beautiful and gentle, a contrast to the drawing of the old man in front of the fire, which was strong and dark, like most of the work; he had come upon it loose, when he was leafing through the sketchbook, and seeing him studying it, Callum had looked up and said briefly, "My dad." With that picture of the dour, exhausted man still firmly in his mind, and this one of the woman with a towel in one hand, balancing and about to step out of the tin bathtub placed in front of the fire, it all fell into place for him. The fireplace and mantel were clearly the same in both drawings, and the woman must be Callum's mother, who, as he remembered from his file, had died when her son was ten. None of the pictures was dated, but Dodds assumed she must have been drawn from memory after her death.

None of this did he mention when he handed back the drawing with a nod to Callum in the trench. The end of a small episode, but certainly not the end of Sergeant Braddis. And Braddis had what Dodds knew he would never have: killer spirit. He should at least leave a memo.

After supper, which consisted of well-prepared warm water from the tap, and nothing else, MacIver pondered the confrontation between the platoon commander and his sergeant. He had been a little surprised at the sexual innuendo creeping into the dialogue. Perhaps it meant nothing: a manly man, as Braddis projected himself to be, might well, with his buddies and in his soul, think all officers soft, and probably homosexual; and in any competition with such people, it might be a good ploy to inject a little taunt along those lines, to soften up a soft

man further, as it were. But *was* Dodds gay? Perhaps, but probably not, MacIver decided, though almost certainly sexually in-
experienced, so who, including himself, could tell? There did
not seem to be many passengers in the *Windrush*, as he plied it
up and down the Broads (unfortunate wording in the context).
At most there would be a few introductions by his mother of
suitable young women ("You really must meet Gwendolyn
Meredith, Linda and Archie's daughter, she's so pretty and kind;
I'll invite her to tea next Thursday"). Simon Dodds, he thought,
knew he wanted more than that, but he certainly had not yet
found her. What about Braddis and Callum, and the nude picture?

MacIver believed that Braddis would have the same attitude
to women as to other possible possessions: he took pretty much
what he pleased, though sex might not rank at the top of his ac-
quisitiveness. MacIver had assumed that Braddis took the picture to contemplate it for his pleasure, even though he left no
mark on it; his use of the word *lewd* indicated that he could find
it arousing, admittedly while acting the puritan. MacIver rated
the chance that Braddis might have been disarmed by the
beauty of the picture at close to zero. And Callum? Callum
knew the picture was beautiful, and he knew it was not lewd, but
that didn't mean that he saw nothing sexual in it. MacIver did
not need Freud to tell him a boy can easily draw both the direction and the shape of his appetite from his mother: why else did
he personally go for high-breasted, slim women who kept their
secrets? But right now, with all his passions somehow turning
like the tide towards yearnings of loss rather than hungers for
gain, he saw a certain poignancy in these three men, each con-
templating this naked woman in the middle of war, and figuring
their separate, private desires around her form; the poignancy, of

course, came from the fact that soon they would all be gone themselves, and all their desires unfulfilled.

And what about Margaret? She taught him that sex did not have to be always intense and fraught. It could be playful.

Soon after they got together, Sally Gordon, flirting busily at a party at her gallery, told MacIver that when she asked Margaret what it was like going to bed with him, she had answered, "It's sort of like going to bed with a polar bear. You know that when he settles down, he's going to keep you nice and snug, but you don't know what sort of friskinesses he's going to get up to first."

"My God, Sally, what did you say?"

"I said I thought I would hate that uncertainty, and she said that she had thought she would hate it too, but it turned out she loved it."

He had leered at Sally horribly; Margaret said that whenever he spoke to her, his Scots burr thickened threefold. "Of course," he said, "Sally is a Gordon," burring fourfold on the *r*'s.

Margaret was ten years younger than he was, but in fact sexually more experienced. He enjoyed teasing her, and tormenting himself, by asking pointed questions about her previous affairs. She was skillful at giving indirect answers to his questions, but at odd times would drop small, precise details of information about this or that encounter, which stirred him into a lather of titillation and jealousy.

"What can you expect?" she said innocently, when not for the first time he had been rendered speechless. "I'm an artist."

"So what?" he retorted. "I'm a rugby player."

"Ooh la-la, a *rugby* player!" she said, feigning terror and laughing delightedly.

In fact, Margaret had liked having a rugby player. Once

when they had been visiting Chelsea, his very English mother had given Margaret a folder she had kept of newspaper cuttings of his games (the fact that she had assembled such a collection astonished him; she had not attended a single one of them at the school, university, club, or international level, until she appeared by good luck with her latest handsome and well-dressed beau at Twickenham on his epic day there; after which, looking radiant, she had hugged him and exclaimed, "O my bonny Scottish boy, what a warrior man you grew to be!"). Margaret took the folder home with her and studied it carefully, and was delighted to find that two different reports of two different games in two different newspapers had referred to him as a "*punishing* runner." And some time later surprised them both at an intense moment of lovemaking by shouting, "Punish me, my strong runner."

She was, in fact, experienced or not, innocent, childlike, and mostly wise. Lying in bed, sometimes after making love, sometimes just playing out their day to each other, he would hold her, half-lying across him, his leg between her thighs, her breast against his chest, her hand up on his shoulder, silk against shag. "Tell me," she would say.

The prick of desire was both distraction and inspiration to him. He told her the story of Angela Trelawney, famous reclusive Cornish painter, and her Bootlegger Cove series: almost a hundred paintings, same cove, but every season and every mood, light, water, rock, maelstrom to brimming calm. One day, within an hour, brisk winds changed to black storm banging in from the horizon, vast seas thundering onto the rocks, spray salting the grasses on the top of the cliffs. While she watched, twenty-four feet of unmasted, blue-hulled sloop suddenly smashed into the point of the northern promontory on the far side of the cove. Instant and total disintegration of boat, and while it was washing away she saw on the next wave a limp figure in a yellow slicker heaved upwards and hurled into the rocks. Margaret always wanted his details; "Paint it," she said, her voice muffled somewhere in his neck.

On with the oilskins. Angela knew every rock in this cove, every roughness and slipperiness. She knew that in a gale like this, if she was to get anywhere near the point, she would have to do it on her knees, and hold on for dear life while every successive wave crashed over her. Not more than eighty yards to the end of the point, but it took her more than ten minutes to get there. Several times she was sure that the water, tearing at her there on the rocks, would prise loose her grip, carry her out into the main surge, and then pound her at leisure like a rag doll on some other chosen rock in the cove.

But finally she got to a raised rock about ten feet above the waterline, the last outcrop before the cove tapered, after millennia of battering, down into the sea itself. Straddling the rock, and clinging to it with arms and knees like a rider dislodged from the saddle onto the neck of a runaway horse, she peered down below her. At once she saw, wedged into a gap in the rocks, the V of the bow and no more than four feet of planking. At first, nothing else. But then, with a shock, she saw the man. He was sprawled face downwards, totally limp, and even as she watched, she saw with horror his left arm float lifelessly upwards on the remnants of a wave as it drained away from the rock.

Was he still alive? She had to get to him to find out. She started counting the number of seconds between the bigger waves, and watched the pattern of their cascade across the rocks where he was lying. She calculated that she would have about six seconds of slack water before she got blasted again; she was lighter than he was: if she missed her moment, she would be swept away like a cork. She waited for two more waves to check her timing. Then on the leeward side, she made her move round the rock, as soon as the water started to slacken.

Six seconds and counting. On hands and knees she crawled to the man, flattened out next to him, her arm across his back, face next to his. "Give me a sign if you hear," she yelled at the top of her voice. "We don't have much time."

An endless wait, without word or movement. Then just as she was about to scuttle back to her rock, a low voice said clearly, "I can hear you." Immediately the next wave crashed over them, and though she was already soaked through, she was not ready for the paralyzing cold and weight of the water crushing her breathless. It seemed longer this time than the six seconds before the water eased. "No more of those if we can help it," she yelled. "Can you move?"

"I don't know," the man said, quicker this time. "We may have to wait out one more wave," she said, "and then we move. Crank every muscle, up around that rock—I'll help." Out of time. The next wave was on them, exacting its punishment.

They weathered that. She gasped for air, grabbed his arm in a vise, and yelled, "NOW!!" He was well built, and she did not know what she would do if he just lay there, but to her relief he was on his feet as quickly as she was, one arm bracing against the rocks. With her pulling on, rather than supporting, the other arm, they lurched up against the tall rock, then slithered round it, quick enough for only their legs to be washed by the next sweeping wave. Propping themselves on the leeward side, they paused for breath. Now she could examine her catch: deadly pale, with a huge, livid contusion, his forehead badly grazed but not bleeding much. Dark eyes, strong mustache, blacker for the pallor around it. "What now?" he said dully.

Once started, MacIver took some stopping. Inch by inch, he told her of their crawl over the slippery higher rocks, their lurching, stumbling run across the top of the cliffs to the cottage ("Don't you dare pass out on me!"), his collapse on passing through the door, her heaping up the fire and undressing herself, her making tea with whisky and honey for both of them, though he had not yet come round, her undressing him and rubbing him hard with towels, to get his circulation going, while admiring his physique, her covering them both with the duvet on the floor in front of the fire for the first round of sleep, her growing concern that he might have a concussion, his revival and reassurance after vomiting and aspirin for his huge headache, his simple inquiry and then gratitude for her having saved his life at risk of her own, and then the second round of sleep, this time with him on the sofa in a large terry-cloth robe under a blanket, and then her second awakening and arousal. MacIver had not missed a beat, and was now in the home stretch, turning the knobs up a little more erotically:

. . . She woke up first, now broad daylight, nine-thirty on the carriage clock, still windy outside, but the storm much reduced, from a bully to a bluster. She was still feeling stiff, but very clear-headed. She could hear his regular breathing from the couch. He had thrown off the blanket in the night, and was lying on his back with the belt of his robe loosely tied. She went and sat on the edge of the sofa, gently undid the belt, and folded back the robe. He was lying peacefully, and the gash on his forehead seemed healthier, though his mustache gave him a stern look. She stroked the hair on his chest, and then let her hand slide downwards and play idly with his pubic hair, and finally slip under his balls. At once she felt things tightening as she maintained her gentle touches, and his lengthening cock started rotating counterclockwise across his thigh, towards a solid twelve o'clock; its tip quivered an inch below his navel. She glanced up to see what effect this was having on the sleeper, and noticed that he hadn't opened his eyes yet, but the mouth under the mustache seemed less severe than before. Indeed, as she watched, the lips parted.

She slipped out of her sweatpants and mounted him, and gave a little gasp of pleasure as she felt him reach inside her. She sat for a moment looking down on him. He opened his eyes.

"Take off that shirt," he said. She did, and it was his turn to look.

"Aren't you lovely?" he said, and began playing with her breasts.

They started moving athletically now, and it was not long before other waves swept over them.

"Have you gone to sleep," MacIver said into Margaret's hair.

"Far from it," she said. "I want to do just what they did."

So they did, and then slept happily and equally deeply, curled together.

Well, thought MacIver, wild nights and wild mornings too; you're certainly allowing yourself some fine, hammy moments. But oh! the lovely depth and easy lassitude of that sleep after love, dearly remembered. Like Orpheus and Eurydice making the long glide down to the Underworld together, always a following wind without resistance. Aristotle says that every animal except woman and the rooster are sad after sex. Speak for yourself, 'Tootles! Shatter the myth. Orpheus-Morpheus. If you pay attention, you can always bring her back with you, every time. Or so he had thought.

So they had good times, each healing whatever hurt the

other had had, almost without noticing it. They were married within a year of their first meeting, on Christmas Eve 1947, and in the next spring, after wonderful sales from Margaret's show, they bought the Night Heron House, to be their summer refuge at the end of the academic year. And just after the fall equinox in 1948, they had their boy, David.

CHAPTER 8

Going Down in the Mud (Part 1)

The worst night yet, the one that promised there would not be many more. A lot of pain, and somehow more constant and diffused, and the fever now also constant, stoked to a high burn and holding. But the worst part was a recurrence of the waves of nausea, which once more drove him to the bathroom for the most painful retching, productive of only very small streams of bile, not enough in some cases to reach the bottom of the basin, but producing great agony through his throat at each surge, which literally drove him to his knees as he stood there. And in the course of the day, there would come another dark dagger of pain, whose beginning he remembered vaguely, but which apparently knocked him sideways off his chair and out, until he came to himself, after God knows how long, lying on the floor. However, the odd thing about all this persecution of him was that, in the periods of intermission from the most violent attacks, he found himself more lucid than he had been in recent months.

He was more determined than ever to press on with his damn story; three days would finish it, and he fully intended to finish it. But today he would invert his procedure. His focus would be the story of his son, David, and he wanted to set the lines of it perfectly straight in his memory: the events here were in his mind the very hub to which everything that happened before was pointed, like spokes that shone brightly out on the perimeter, but darkened as they approached the center. And everything that followed seemed somberly colored in his mind, in mood and significance. It was not that he was never happy again; he had just lost the expectation of happiness, so that his memories of his son and of what happened to him came to serve as categories of grief, rage, yearning, through which everything else would pass. Thus the dark side of MacIver's nature was re-inforced by the death of David. The young men would enter their last battle in the grim light of what he had learned from his early fallen child.

David MacIver, a quick and blithe spirit, Ariel light, took after his mother physically, and in much of her gentle under-standing of things, though he had and showed his father's tem-per from an early age, and the same way of reaching a sticking point of stubbornness. He produced the same range of vivid expression of all small children who observe closely and like to play with words ("Why does Mickey Mouse have a squash ball for a nose?"), but could lose himself happily like his mother for hours on end with a crayon in his hand. ("What is that a picture of, David?" "It's not a picture. I'm making color marks, to see which ones I like best.")

As he grew up, thin as a rail, he became a graceful athlete, taking to games MacIver never played, like tennis and baseball. MacIver cleared some more ground to the side of the woods, so they could have fielding practice; he might not play baseball, but he had at least a good arm, having thrown the javelin for Oxford in his off-season. ("Do you have good technique?" his rugby friend Terry asked. "Fuck technique, Terry. It's amazing how far you can make the thing go, if you imagine someone you really dislike on the receiving end.") Between them, father and son evolved a game of graded difficulty in fielding, to be played each summer evening before supper. They would begin with the Tame Bunnies, essentially simple warm-up pitches, in which Margaret was invited to participate—she always declined. At the further end were the Zingeraccis (fast balls), the Hairy Pops (major-league pop-ups), and the Wild Wicked Ones (difficult grounders, delivered at pace, and bouncing with great irregularity on the uneven ground). MacIver always threw, and David always fielded. He would have the right to order up à la carte the number of each kind of throw he wanted to receive, "eight Zs, Dad, six HPs, and another eight WWOs," and the point of the game was for him to have an error-proof round, including the throw back to his father, who refused to stretch more than two feet in any direction. Which is where some ugliness would enter, the father pigheaded for perfection, the son not beyond patronizing: "You've never played this game, Dad, you don't know: ask anyone who does, and he would say that I almost made an impossible play, and that in fact it was an unreachable ball, and no error." Sometimes Margaret would be appealed to, but she would rebuff them. "You're as bad as each other. If a Martian watched the two of you playing games, and was asked at the end what he thought *sportsmanship* meant, he would have to say that it was the art of taking weaselly advantage of one's opponent."

Inside, however, Margaret held sway and peace reigned. The lovely meals, not just delicious by the mouthful, but so graceful in the setting and serving, lulled the house down to calmness; good talk around the table—the day, the work and the joke, sports, politics, film, music, art, people—a bonded trio, listening to each other. Again, the boy and his dad would have good times, with every sort of chat, while they did the dishes, and then very often the three of them would read to each other, first children's classics, and later a wider sweep of novels and poetry, and sometimes all of them taking parts in plays. Margaret's beauty cast its spell, and so did her voice. "Read some more, Mom," David would say, when she paused; and MacIver would second him: "Yes, do, love." They were both in love with her.

Everything went on, it seemed, in easy rhythms, even in New York in their Riverside Drive apartment, even through the teenage years. Try as he might, MacIver could not recall phases of tantrums, of rebellion, even of acne in the boy. David did well in school and seemed well liked. The girls he brought home were all beautiful, slim and graceful with gorgeous hair and quiet measured voices. MacIver was staggered at this profusion of grace: "Goddammit," he said in bed, "he brings home nothing but your daughters." "I certainly wish they were," said Margaret. "Perhaps we could adopt them all."

But the bubble of the idyll, if that's what it was, was pricked on a point of principle, so devastating in its outcome that MacIver could never fully believe in the possibility of *real* happiness ever again. David had spent three semesters at Yale, liking the place and pondering the questions on war and race; he did not like so much the bowwow theater around the questions, the effigy burning, the slogan bashing, or even the big set-pieces, the austere Kingman Brewster on the Green, the eloquent and humorous William Sloane Coffin in the Chapel, but he liked finding the beginnings of stirring and shaping, perhaps for the first time in his life, actual convictions—not just gut feelings— among his friends and, more important, further down, in his own soul. He was waiting for the still, small voice, like Elijah at the mouth of the cave. The war was easy—who would not repudiate the bully-boy rectitude, the beef-fed certainties about the good we could do for this poor country and many others, shoring up the dominoes, whether we spoke their languages or not, the parade march of ignorance and arrogance once more in step behind the hardware? But there was the missing piece— what about those herded against their will into the swamps, the featureless estuaries, the booby-trapped jungle paths to work their country's will so stated? Never been away from home before, most of them. "I got nothin' against them Cong." All these were victims too.

One day in Sterling Library, with a rally going on outside, slightly muffled by several thicknesses of neo-Gothic stone, he came upon a tattered copy of the Welsh poet and artist David Jones's *In Parenthesis,* the difficult prose poem he wrote about his own experiences in World War I, the great folly that set the century reeling on its catastrophic way. The war, David remembered, in which his unknown grandfather was killed, and his father's chosen field. The poem, which David found difficult in its allusiveness, is dedicated in a beautiful inscription:

THIS WRITING IS FOR MY FRIENDS IN MIND OF
ALL COMMON AND HIDDEN MEN AND OF THE
SECRET PRINCES . . . AND TO THE ENEMY FRONT-
FIGHTERS WHO SHARED OUR PAINS
AGAINST WHOM WE FOUND OURSELVES
BY MISADVENTURE.

And at the back of the book is a drawing of a young ram, with a delicate face, standing transfixed by a bent spear and enmeshed in barbed wire; on the facing page quotations mostly from the Old Testament, but leading with Revelations 5:6 in Latin, *Et vidi . . . agnum stantem tamquam occisum,* which David could translate: I saw the lamb standing, as though slain. . . . He saw the wealth of imagery in the lines of the drawing, going back to Abraham and the ram caught by his horns in a thicket of thorns, who would die for Isaac, and forward to Jesus, the Lamb of God, who would die for the sins of the world—the whole notion of the scapegoat and the old simile "sent like a lamb to the slaughter." David looked and looked, and a determination grew inside him.

And the next day he saw something that sealed it ineradicably in place. He was walking down Chapel Street and passing York, when he looked down and saw there had been a terrible crash—a truck had almost demolished a small car, which was on fire. He walked towards it. An ambulance and a fire truck were there, and there was clearly an urgency: the car's gas tank might well explode soon, and there was someone still in the car. While he watched, an enormous black fireman—a rarity in himself—seized the buckled door on the driver's side, ripped it off its crippled hinges, and threw it aside. Then quietly to the hovering ambulance men, he said, "Set the stretcher right here at full height," indicating a position just behind him parallel to the car. "We've got to be careful—I think his back may be broken." Without more ado, he reached into the car, sliding his right arm behind the man's back and under him, keeping it as straight as possible as a kind of splint, then cradling his legs with his left arm, and seemingly effortlessly lifting him free of the car, as though he were a child, and laying him very tenderly on the stretcher behind him. The man had moaned softly once, and the fireman had said gently, "It'll be all right, sir." Then the small chorus of *Well done*s, and a nod from the fireman as he returned to his engine, while his mates proceeded to blast the car with foam and water and extinguished the blaze before it could explode.

But as he walked away from the scene, only one thought was hammering in David's head: "That fireman may well have a son, as unquestionably hundreds of thousands of mothers and fathers do, without a student deferment, who is in Vietnam right now, without ever having wanted to be there, and who deserves every bit as much devoted service as that fireman just gave." And there and then he resolved that he would go to Vietnam as a medic; he would not lawyer it up, he would not play the new lottery number game, he would not even seek the status of conscientious objector: he would join the medical corps if they would have him, and as soon as they would have him.

He phoned Margaret up and said that he would be coming home the next day, and that he had made a big decision. "I have felt this coming," she said, "though I am fairly sure your father hasn't. Come home." He went home, and they sat talking about it deep into the night. The trouble was they could not argue with any sort of principle on the other side to his, except the almost unutterable principle of their fear of losing him. They tried to urge on him that he would certainly give his life to service, but he did not have to give it this instant; he could prepare himself in any number of useful ways right now, and give a lifetime of necessary and specialized service to untold numbers of people. Why now? Anything to buy time. But he had answered that the emergency was now, and it came earmarked for his own peers and age group, and he must meet it now, or despise himself. As the conversation went on, MacIver felt he had less and less to say. Noticing his glumness across the table, David came round and hugged him: "It's all right, Dad, I'm not going to get killed."

"That's what my father told me," said MacIver, and before he could help himself, tears were pouring down his face. When he'd managed to gather himself, he said, "I don't want you to feel bad, but you should know those tears were not for my father."

"I know, Dad, I know. But I will be back." Hugging him again.

Later, finally in bed and holding each other, Margaret said: "It's probably our fault: we wanted him to be good, and he's just turning out to be better than we wanted."

The next day things cheered up a bit. The two men went north in the big Oldsmobile station wagon to bring home David's stuff. They had urged Margaret to come, but she declined.

"Come on, Mom, you can do the judgment of Solomon on what we bring back and what we give away."

"I'll leave the two of you to argue that out. I'll be making a wonderful supper for you both here. Be back by seven-thirty."

David drove, and MacIver lounged in the corner of the big front seat, looking back towards his son. The boy said he was worried about his greenness—that he would find himself for the first time in the presence of something truly shocking, and simply freeze instead of immediately engaging with the problem.

"That won't happen with you, and I've worked out why," said MacIver. "I was once in a car crash—nothing like as bad as the one you described last night—in the thirties sometime, when I was doing my Ph.D. I was not badly hurt, but I didn't function properly, and I worried about it right into World War Two."

"What happened?"

"It was late November, I think, thin drizzle close to freezing, fall having an early stab at winter. I was somewhere near Danbury, probably on what became big Route 84, but then just a well-traveled road through the country. I was going too fast, conscious of having difficulty holding the car to the road— skinny little tires back then, remember. I'm on a right-hand bend up onto a bridge, and as I reach the top, bingo, there's a stationary oil truck, which has clearly been having the same difficulties, spanning pretty much the whole roadway not twenty yards ahead.

"Jam on the brakes, and in the screaming sideways glide out of control, I know I'm going to hit the truck. So afterwards I wonder, if I hadn't frozen and seized, as the brakes had, whether I could not have snuck the car more maneuverably round the back end of the thing. The corner of my eye detected a small gap, but my reflexes couldn't take me there; somehow the car and I were together magnetized or attracted to the predicament of the laborious damn truck. There were impressions and questions, I remembered afterwards, flicking through the mind, like—*oil*-truck: conflagration? *Hit tires rather than truck's metal body:* more forgiving. *Blind curve:* pileup from traffic behind? In the event, I could do nothing; I sat there and let it all happen."

"How bad was it?"

"Not so bad, really. The car somehow slid parallel to the truck and, with the brakes locked, kept closing on it, my guess is still doing about forty. It hit half against a tire and half into metal ahead of it, and seemed to ride up and then tilt back to the right from its momentum. The driver's door was banged in about half a seat's width, and I ended up in the middle of the car with some impressive bruises down my left side. Windshield cascaded past me leftwards in a shower of glass, and two pieces gashed the back of my right hand and my forehead on their way by. But I wasn't trapped in any way—I was able to crawl out the door on the passenger side, and face the music. Spookily quiet, I remember; the engine had been slammed off on impact, I suppose: just dripping sounds from various liquids seeping onto the road. No pileup: drivers behind driving more sensibly able to stop.

"But again I did not function—I registered impressions in a disengaged sort of way, with the sound switched off. People led me over to the side of the road. An ambulance man patched up my forehead and stopped the blood draining into my left eye, as it had been doing. A fire truck arrived and sprayed foam on my car and the road around it. Various police cars at irregular angles pulsing blue lights into the evening. Hefty, tattooed driver of the truck, looking a little distant himself, kept repeating, like some kind of saving mantra, 'You came up too fast.' And I said, 'I didn't expect to see you there,' which was greeted approvingly as some kind of laconic witticism, but I was out of it. I got no details; when they took me off to hospital to stitch me up, and observe me for concussion overnight, I knew nothing—where the truck driver was from, what license number, what company, what make, year, color of truck, what insurance—nothing. The police, who see many worse things every day, had all the details, but I had nothing."

"So why won't that happen to me, when I go into the crunch?"

"Yes, that's the question, and I kept asking it of myself: why won't it happen again, when the big guns go off in the navy, and the killing starts? And the answer I found is that it doesn't happen to you when you're in a situation of responsibility for others; there the button is pressed that has you scurrying for answers to

the problems besetting your group, under great compulsion—
I must make this better for us. But when you are on your own,
interestingly, it seems to me, self-preservation, if anything, mag-
nifies the enormity of the threats to oneself, and that seems to
invite the freeze—you have no part in any wider context to re-
duce it all to proportion, or to get something happening. You
can simply sit and become the rabbit in the headlights."

"Dad, you should have been a psychologist."

"Yeah, right. Anyway, my bet for what it's worth is that you'll
never freeze, so forget about it."

"Do you think also that sometimes, the level of expectations
directed towards you compels you to rise higher, to be more than
yourself?"

"Yes, I do."

"Thinking of Mom and you will keep me on my mettle."

"So will thinking of your fireman's son, as you told us yesterday."

"Yes."

The cleanup at Yale went much faster than MacIver expected. And there was much less for old Big Blue to carry back
with them, in part because David gave a lot of very nice things
to his friends, who had come by in large numbers to wish him
well. The mood, MacIver thought, taking its temperature, was
quieter than the normal undergraduate gathering; "warm but
subdued," he decided. He used the same sort of oxymoron when
a young man asked him how he felt about David's decision, and
he replied, "I suppose unhappy about it and proud of it, if the
two can go together," and the young man had looked at him a
little sadly, and said that it was the perfect description of how
they were all feeling, except that in his own case he would have
to add the tag "ashamed of myself." And MacIver said, to ease

his embarrassment, "No, no, lad. The hard, painful decisions have to be taken in one's own time; you'll make them when you're ready."

The dinner was as good as Margaret had promised, the mood quite close to the Yale dormitory's, though there was more laughter. And in the intervening days, everything moved along exactly as David would have wished. Yes, he could sign up for the medical corps, pending a physical and some other tests for suitability. And yes, he could request, and was likely to be granted, service in Vietnam; that was currently the area of greatest need. And for Margaret and MacIver there was the temporary relief that after boot camp at Fort Dix the medical training would be conducted at Brooke Army Medical Center in Texas, and the interval between first enlistment and posting would be five to six months. The mills of the military, as MacIver remembered, grind as slowly as those of God, but just as inexorably.

The next intake for the medical corps was scheduled for April 6, a little more than three weeks away; he should move very fast, if he wanted to be included in it. The one after would be at the end of May. He made the April date, of course, and after Fort Dix was off to Texas. Margaret and MacIver met him twice in San Antonio and once in Austin on his weekend leaves over the summer, and he came home for a final four days before leaving for Vietnam on October 8, 1968, ten days after his twentieth birthday, and precisely a week after his father's sixty-second. On this last trip, they both noticed a more serious set of mind, even more determined, with his eye always on the distant object, but also, MacIver thought, undistractible from his anxieties. Even while still in America, David had seen clearly that ardor was a discounted value in the army ("Just do it by the book, soldier"); it would become even more so in the field

("Cool the gung ho, buddy; carry on like this, and you're going to get us all killed").

So MacIver, the military historian, was back in the business of reading letters home, but in this case, of course, letters read and scrutinized for every nuance with an intensity he had never mustered before. And they were wonderful letters. The description of the base, the insulated bastion of home away from home, where familiar music plays over and over from the speakers and the menu does its crazy dance through everyone's ethnic food. There was interdivisional baseball, and David played shortstop for the medics. ("We have *real* umpires here, Dad, so of course no errors on the shortstop!") And then the telling of explorations farther afield, the temple, the market, the children's fishing pool for carp, and the lovely gifts sent home—a silk shawl of heraldic colored birds passing through branches, for Margaret's birthday, and for MacIver on Father's Day, a beautiful lacquered bowl, gold within, jade colored on the outside, with two panels on opposite sides showing herons, very finely drawn and subtly different, fishing among reeds on a lake. He was telling them he was thinking of them and the Wellfleet house.

There was a simple progression of escalating danger for the medics—base hospital, field hospital, assignment to soldiers' units in the field, and then medevac helicopter personnel, rescuing the wounded from the battlefield itself. They knew he would not rest till he was in the helicopters. As Margaret said, "He's not just testing himself, he's determined to place himself on precisely the same ground as his fireman and the injured man in the burning car about to explode. I don't mind telling you, I pray every day to anyone out there that this will not be the day."

The phone call came on July 3 at nine-fifteen in the morning, and Margaret picked up; MacIver was out running.

"Mrs. MacIver?"

A tremulous yes.

"Mrs. MacIver, my name is Stafford Dionne, and I'm a friend of David's, and he asked me to make this call. He's a little groggy right now, because he's taken a hit, but he's going to be fine. The hard thing I have to tell you is that he's lost the lower half of his right leg just above the knee, but they've saved the rest of the leg, and they have no doubt that he will heal up well. He lost a lot of blood, and he's also picked up a fever, so they're working on getting the fever down and the blood level up to normal. He's groggy now mostly from the aftereffects of the surgery and anesthesia, but he will be much more himself, I am sure, in two days. So I will phone you again tomorrow about the same time if that's all right, to tell you how he's getting along, and the day after that, my guess is, he'll be calling you himself. Are you okay, Mrs. MacIver?"

"Yes, thank you, Stafford, I'm sort of pulling myself together here; it's awful but in a sense it's a relief. . . . It's so much less than we feared. Do you know what happened and when?"

"Yes, it was about four o'clock in the afternoon out here two days ago, so that would make it early yesterday morning on your clock. Exactly what happened is hard to say in this sort of situation. You fly in low over the trees taking fire, you land in a clearing taking fire while you pick up casualties, and then as fast as you can, you take off still under fire. Dave was on the ground loading stretchers when he got hit, but we will probably never know by what—could have been a mortar round, a piece of shrapnel, a buried mine being exploded nearby. There's always a lot happening in those situations, a lot of yelling and a lot of dust in the air from the chopper blades."

"They fire on medical planes and personnel?"

"I'm afraid they do. I'm afraid this is not a war on either side where people keep a copy of the Geneva convention in their pockets."

"Are you a medic, too, Stafford? And where are you from?"

"I'm a helicopter pilot, ma'am, from Oakland, California. Dave and I work a lot together."

"He's very lucky to have you as a friend. Are you all right yourself?"

"I'm just fine, Mrs. MacIver, and so will my buddy be. I look forward to talking to you again tomorrow, and hope we can all meet sometime real soon. You can tell your husband that I try to play a little rugby, but I'll never be up to his level."

"I'll tell him," said Margaret, "but I know what he would say: 'You're the helicopter pilot who saved my son, and I was just a piddling center for Scotland.' Thank you more than I can say, Stafford, and God bless you."

"You're very gracious, ma'am. Speak to you tomorrow. Good-bye now."

Next morning the phone rang at nine-twenty and MacIver, as they had agreed, picked it up. Stafford on the other end, his voice audibly upbeat: "Mr. MacIver? I have a surprise for you both," and he handed the receiver to David, who sounded a little quiet, but firm and fully himself.

So they got him back, and the price was high, though there had been many days, they knew, when they would have told each other that *no* price would be too high, as long as they got him back. But it seemed afterwards that he was only grudgingly given back. The fever had turned out to be far more obdurate than anyone had warned them, and in fact its cause was never diagnosed. Eventually in September he had been well enough to be moved to a hospital in Hawaii, which had seemed the perfect halfway house for a jaunty reunion, but the sun was dimmed for them when they saw how wasted he was—not just wounded, and they had tried to prepare themselves for the sight of it, but clearly still unwell.

Three weeks in Hawaii seemed to put the fever behind him, and he was moved to a new orthopedic ward set up for physiotherapy at the Kingsbridge VA hospital in the Bronx. Good for easy visiting, and in fact they all celebrated both David's birthday on the twenty-ninth there and MacIver's on October 1. The boy had almost come home. A few days after that on a Saturday, MacIver, who had always been good at working bureaucratic fiddles, had arranged with both hospital authorities and the head office of the city water supply to take David, the returned wounded veteran, in a wheelchair down Sedgwick Avenue and up to the big reservoir at the far end, where they would be admitted to the perimeter track beside the water for some birdwatching. Good for his morale, everyone had agreed, and was happy to collaborate. Margaret and he had always visited him together, but for this she suggested he do it alone. "I think there may well be things he wants to talk about," she said, "but to protect me from."

"What sort of things?" said MacIver, instantly alarmed.

"I can't give you an agenda, but perhaps pain, for one," she said.

It was the perfect day for the visit, at the heart of the migratory season, when waterbirds in large numbers would be using this sanctuary for a staging ground before their long flights south. A completely still afternoon, with a ribbed canopy of cloud like a scallop shell held motionless overhead, so hushed and windless that on Sedgwick Avenue you could hear ragged cheers rising from Baker Field at the tip of Manhattan a couple of miles away—Columbia bravely supporting another mismatched football team.

MacIver had lived on Sedgwick Avenue as a graduate student more than thirty-five years before, poised for a plunge down the hill to the IRT at 231st Street, and remembered how the icy wind could hone that crest in winter, sharpening the bulk of the ugly old hospital into still more ascetic lines. But now all was mildness. Everything had been very affable as they set out, nurses busying with rugs around the chair, pressing bread for the ducks on them. Up Sedgwick Avenue, the quiet fall Saturday, boys in sneakers leaning idly against the cars, past the Catholic church and the playground. They were quite at ease with each other, no need to talk but no difficulty about saying anything they felt like, either. MacIver was moved by time taking him back—from the stroller to the wheelchair, the old feeling of the weight on the arms, taking longish steps to get a low center of gravity.

Down alongside the reservoir, where the slim maples and plane trees had buckled the concrete path with the vigor of their roots. Then cut through the playground at the far end, up the hill again and through the gatehouse. As promised, there was a genial Guardian of the Water there to let them in, who was very deferential to David. This was going to be a good afternoon. No glare on the surface of the water, but enough light to make large reflections, and smooth as pewter.

They went a little way around the side, and MacIver sat on the grass beside him, and gave him the binoculars. Scaups and canvasbacks for the most part, but some mallards too, and two pairs of Canada geese with a Westchester look about them—lost their bearings, no doubt. That elegiac feeling of Indian summer, no chill, but the sap and the life quietly seeping out of things, under the distant monochrome arch of sky.

They talked about the war, and whatever anger there had been seemed to have been bled out of the boy. "A complete make-believe world," he said. "No good railing against this distortion of news, that cover-up. Whole thing so misconceived, so many spokesmen warping the turn of events, that even the planners probably ended up duping themselves, and therefore to some extent sincere. All the more dangerous because they believed their own shit."

They sat a long time. Every now and again a pair of ducks would come in to land on the reservoir, their lovely long-necked, fast-drumming flight, and then the wing-back, down-tailed braking onto the smooth surface. Sometimes a few quick scudding motions, as intruders were chased out of claimed territories. The ripples from these little turbulences lapped ever so gently on the stone wall below them. They absentmindedly ate some pieces of the bread the nurses had given them, and then, to complete the necessary rituals of childhood, threw some onto the water to bring the ducks closer. Eventually, a small detachment of mallards and scaups swam lazily over to indulge them, and they paused in their talk to admire once more the beautiful livery of their uniform markings.

MacIver asked about the pain of his ordeal, but David had pretty much put that behind him, too. Occasional echoes of it would run through his body, or tug at his unsightly amputation, but he was not going to linger on the memory of its full rampage. "It owns you, and it's determined to kill you," he said, "and the longer it lasts, the further you can feel it pushing you away from any contact with the world or with living. A sense of reprieve when it recedes—reprieved and somehow innocent. Innocent and weak, like children; in this case, all one's strength and evil purged away together."

"What does he know of evil?" thought MacIver sadly, but did not say.

It was starting to get dark when they headed back. The motionless leaves above the path stood out black against the deepening sky, except under the streetlights, whose amber glow lent them some almost tropical greens and yellows. The lights from the Lehman College library beat across the water strongly to them.

On the way back, David was so silent, MacIver thought he was asleep. He seemed to have sunk down into the chair. Suddenly, out of nowhere, he said they had decided he needed another operation on his stump. A piece of jagged bone was disturbing the nerve tissue and preventing healing, and they could not fit him with a prosthesis with it in that condition. It would be a relatively simple operation, and would set him up for full mobility before Christmas came.

The operation was done at the end of the next week, in a big city hospital by a distinguished orthopedic surgeon, who was also a consultant for the Kingsbridge hospital and was thoroughly familiar with David's case. The operation went as routinely as the surgeon had said it would, and David was back in his room before lunchtime. Margaret and MacIver visited him again that evening, and found him looking well, and of very high morale: the dreaded onslaught of pain, which he had been waiting for since he left the recovery room, had clocked in so far at a much reduced and more tolerable level than he had let himself hope for; he would be all right now.

This time the phone call came at 7:35 the next morning. A

nurse making a routine check at 4:30 had found David dead in his room; an embolism had formed in his wound and moved to the heart. There had been a frantic effort to revive him after the fact, but he was dead. MacIver took the call, and he and Margaret were at the hospital soon after eight. And here they were the victims of a large and humiliating bureaucratic error. On arrival they went straight to David's room: he was not there—in fact, there were two hospital orderlies cleaning out his effects and making up the room. They had been told it was urgently required for another early-morning admittance. Inquiries revealed that David had been taken down to an operating theater a while before. Sleepy ward nurses, coming to the end of their shift after a harried night, started to make anxious calls. He was no longer in any of the operating theaters or recovery rooms. By now a hospital administrator was hovering with expressions of concern.

David's body was finally located in the hospital's morgue. MacIver happened to be by the phone when this piece of information was reported at the nurse's station. They said they would bring the body back to the room. It was by now 8:55, and MacIver's fury was approaching white heat; he insisted that they would not tolerate any further delay ("will not risk our son's being lost again in an elevator or corridor"), and demanded that they be taken directly to the morgue. Panicky reversal of decision—"No, don't bring it up; they're coming down"—and even more clucking from the administrator. Margaret, in her grief, could not restrain her husband.

He had made a mistake, and he realized it. The body was lying on a steel gurney in the appalling, crude room when they came in. The sheet that had been covering him had apparently been bloodstained, and they were in the process of changing it.

They were brought to a halt by the spectacle: Margaret gave a little cry and buried her head against MacIver's coat; her sobs and shuddering were shaking him to the bone. "O my love," he said, "I am so, so sorry."

But true to himself, he had to make himself look: the young body, the pathetic, wasted stump of a leg livid in color, with iodine stains along the track of the stitches. His head tilted back, arrested in a distorted, straining position with neck muscles tense (perhaps they had been doing something at the back of his head, or rigor setting in), one day's growth of boy's beard shadowing his jaw. His penis rested on the top of his thigh; not much hair on his body. MacIver had no idea what lovers he had had, if any, but caught himself reassuring himself irrelevantly, thinking, "He was a gentle boy; he would be a gentle lover." The administrator nervously mentioned that he might want to talk to someone about arrangements. MacIver gave him a long look, and then said quietly: "Take care of him. Don't lose him again. If you give me the right number, I'll call about arrangements." He took down the number. Below him, still shaking, Margaret said, "You must take me away; oh, oh—that he should have come home to this." As they clung to each other through the night, she whispered to him, "What is going to happen to us now?"

CHAPTER 9

Going Down in the Mud (Part 2)

MacIver had in memory conducted his son once more to his death, and was now sure what few further steps he and his story must take to reach a parallel end. The tartan rug wrapped like a sarong twice around his waist on top of the sweatpants, and the faded Wasps rugby cap down low over his eyes for the most focused view of the page, he advanced on his old machine and wrote:

Sergeant Braddis believed himself a lucky man, with an almost religious belief—that is, he had a steady conviction that whatever dark divinity presided over his destiny, it would provide him with the chances to do what he had to do. Right now, he knew he badly needed an offensive. So of course did his general HQ, so we should not assume that one sergeant unilaterally moved the stars in his favor. In fact, the high command on both sides, having maneuvered hundreds of thousands of men and tons of matériel into the thickest gridlock in history, knew they had to make a move now and again, to show their supporters that, if they could not dislodge it, they could still make some progress within it. To this end, thousands of men on both sides were routinely killed for the gain of a hundred yards or less between the lines, the change suddenly perceived from the map to offer crucial strategic advantages—a straighter line of communication and a shorter trench to defend, or a better surveillance point and gun mounting at the northern end of the line; whoever got the Pope's Nose or Rudy's Corner would be in a position to make large gains. Often the generals on the two sides saw as one on these matters, so crucial positions might be yielded and taken back more than once in the course of weeks.

The strategic niceties were not for Braddis; what he needed was some immediate action, of any kind at all, and on the day after Callum was given his picture back by Dodds, he got some. The previous afternoon the mysterious rumor mill had been working overtime, with subtly various reports that they would be going over the top for this or that purpose, but nothing developed. Mess kits prepared for the morrow with rations and water bottle in the pack, however, and early bed and Last Post meant they were wrong only about the time. And well before dawn, the great orchestral warm-up began, played only by percussion, as the big guns behind the British trenches started their concerted pounding, and had the men up and readying themselves. Wherever they were going, they would advance, at least in theory, safely behind the steel curtain of large-shelled detonations moving ahead of them, forcing the enemy to keep its head down in its deepest bunkers. From the fire-step you could see the tall white, orange, and black plumes soar up, a seething but shapely instant forest-screen of destruction, compounded of mud, smoke, metal, and explosive chemicals. Pray God, when the time came, the gunners would keep the range and the speed of the advance right, and not bury their own men in the craters they would dig.

Lieutenant Dodds had found out early, when he had been on the receiving end of German artillery, that it did not matter much, for purposes of actual fighting, whether you were hit or not. The fact was, after as much as three hours of a barrage, you were softened into a curious quiescence, as though your spirit recoiled and withdrew its open face on the world to some private place in the center of you; people who had been under heavy shelling for a while offered much less resistance when the enemy actually appeared at their trench ready to fight. Dodds had noticed that Braddis wore earplugs whenever the guns opened up, and had adopted the practice himself, and found that he retained a much higher level of alertness. He hoped the Germans had been slow getting the word on the earplugs, and that their ears were at least as sensitive to loud cacophonous noise as his— they were meant to love music, after all.

The plan for the day was on a larger scale than recent ones had been. At the northern end of this sector, the trench system moved forward more than seventy meters to include a small grove (Sammy's Copse) on raised ground, long since denuded of any trees, but with a good vantage point on the tormented fields below. The orders were that they should advance the whole front line the requisite eighty meters to incorporate the copse fully into a flush system with trenches around the base of the knoll, and allow for the addition of various other angled fire-bays, so that any advance against the line would then be subject to fire from different directions. Both companies of the Norfolks and all their platoons were to be involved in the work. They would secure the terrain, they would dig in, and by nightfall they would be firmly if not cosily settled, eighty meters closer to their enemy.

"It's meant to be an upgraded, rational system," said Dodds.

"It's a fuckin' lot of work, is what it is, beggin' your pardon, sir," said Braddis.

"It's certainly that."

"And will the Germans come out and eat their sandwiches and watch us dig, and offer a few tips on our construction? Very tidy bunker-builders, they are, the Germans."

"Perhaps if we take some beer along for them."

"Oh, yes, sir, please, sir. They'll love that. Very matey it'll be for all of us."

The Norfolks moved over the top at 0620, the sun long up on a warm spring day. Lieutenant Dodds led Section 2 of his platoon in the center, with Sergeant Braddis off to his right leading Section 1, and Private Charles Alston in charge of Section 3 on the left, the senior private taking over for Corporal Nicholson, who had been hit by a sniper in the shoulder two weeks before and invalided home. From the start it was clear it would not be the proverbial walk in the park; two men were down before they had gone thirty yards. You cannot send as noisy an advertisement as a morning's barrage without alerting many people that something else may be about to happen. The Germans were out and about, apparently in at least as large numbers as the Norfolks, probably having calculated that they would be safer on the far side of the heavy shelling, mixing it with the English infantry and their small arms, than waiting at home to be buried by repeated rounds of 250 pounds of explosive designed to excavate deeper than your house.

In the confusion that developed, Dodds had to attend to the deployment of his section, but as always on these advances, the corner of his eye was constantly being caught by the athletic figure of Braddis in motion off to the right, light on his feet, landing always in balance on the levelest, firmest, driest patch of ground among the loosely connected web of declivities, puddles, potholes, and depthless craters of the drowned landscape of no-man's-land. A flick of the finger to his waiting section to join him, having shown them the way. They would scurry across to him as to their only pillar of salvation. And Dodds saw it was not just fast and balanced feet, but quickness of eye, and an uncanny kind of three-dimensional awareness of where he stood in the terrain, that made the man a prince of Braddis Land. Traversing the inside of a crater, using its rim for cover, he never lost speed, but as the uneven rim rose and dipped above him, without calculation he would adjust his bend of knee and waist so he was never exposed; and when a German head suddenly appeared over the top of the crater, looking down on this nest of Englanders, Braddis was looking to the right place and blew it away, a cartridge always in the breech, as though he were in an arcade shooting gallery, before the man could bring his gun up.

Dodds was always in wonderment at these displays of the skills of war. Once when they were on the firing range at their training depot outside Norwich, he remembered watching Braddis taking the men through their paces—the particular exercise, snap shooting with regular ammunition from the sandbags at eighty yards, ten shots in ten seconds. He was a known quantity in this department, recognized as one of the top ten marksmen in the British army, silver cups won at Bisley and so on. Some of the men labored, especially two or three left-handers who had to handle the bolt on the right side ("What's the matter with you?" Braddis yelled with his boot resting on the backside of a prone rifleman, who still had two shots to go after the bell; and hearing the reason, added witheringly, "The army

doesn't cater for freaks!"). Others were quite good, especially
Charles Alston, the gamekeeper, as you would expect; not fast,
but accurate, eight bulls out of ten. Then Braddis himself took
his own lovingly maintained rifle, settled at the sandbag, and ran
off a swift procession of bulls in about half the permitted time,
the wooden pointer down at the target barely keeping up with
each immaculate shot. And after he had completed his ten in a
row, he had an eleventh cartridge ready for the pointer itself, and
exploded it as it reached towards the red circle in the center. And
Dodds remembered having noted to himself with astonishment:
This is a man who is never fully himself unless he's at war. (Yes,
MacIver thought: we still meet his kind, and often we admire
him. God help me, sometimes I admire him, not his general so
often, but the expert fighting man himself. Three thousand
years and more after the Trojan War, it's still possible to show an
Achilles at home guiding his reluctant men through his own
private Hades.)

By the afternoon, it was clear that the Norfolks could not
keep the sliver of land they had "taken," or rather advanced over:
it was no-man's-land after all, less than eighty yards of it, and
three dead of thirty and another six wounded was the cost of
their passage. Other platoons, especially in the other company,
had fared worse, it turned out, and by 1300 hours there were
runners passing between the various sectors of engagement, taking the pulse of a failing effort by counting the casualties. If they
were too thinly spread to dig in, then why were they still there?
The authors of the plan, of course, were reluctant to abort it—
the fault could not *be* in the plan—and it was only after each
company commander in turn had pointed out that if the numbers were further whittled away, it might well entail the loss not
just of the narrow slice of land they had "gained" in the morning

but of the trenches from which they had started. A little egg on your face is not as bad as the whole omelette in your face. They were on the verge of inviting their enemy to sit down at their table with them.

Dodds would wait till the order to withdraw was given, but he would not endanger his men further, constantly in movement in search of some mythical defensible line. He had his section hunker down along the wall of a crater, conveniently crenellated by previous fighting, but offering both some protection and a view of the approaches from the German lines. He had Braddis and Alston join him. "We can't dig in here. We're out of touch with the other platoons, not to mention the other company and whoever else is trying to mark off their section of this new trench line. It might work if we had an armistice and someone with a very long tape and a big megaphone making it all straight. But as it is, with those we've lost already, we certainly can't both hold a line and afford the trenchers to do their work at the same time. We should quickly find the safest protected stretch of terrain to allow us to keep all three sections in touch with each other, and hold it until we get the order to move back."

"Correct decision, sir, if you'll allow me," said Braddis. "An isolated pocket of trenches built as a monument to a mess of bodies of its diggers is not going to help anyone. You seem to be pretty well settled here, sir, and Section 1 can do as well just off to the right over there."

"How about you, Charles?" said Dodds.

"Section 3 will certainly welcome the decision, sir," Alston said. "We've sent two back killed and another four wounded besides already. But we're quite nicely placed where we are now, and can hold on a while."

The order to withdraw came an hour and a half later: "Immediate orderly withdrawal to front positions. Platoon commanders report to battalion HQ at 1700 hours." They heard afterwards that close to Sammy's Copse, militarily perhaps the one desirable feature in this otherwise featureless terrain, the line had buckled quite early, and reinforcements had to be rushed forward to shore it up. There had been no question of a forward extension from the start. But once settled, Dodds's platoon on the neglected south end of the line had little trouble holding their ground over the interval. The Germans had brought up a light machine gun on their far right, which could have spelled havoc, but before they could even get its legs firmly bedded, Braddis, moving low and smartly to the right, had lobbed a grenade precisely among them and finished their effort. The German resolve had seemed to falter at that point; they ebbed away, perhaps even recalled back to their lines in a more timely fashion than the No. 3 Platoon of Company A of the Norfolks.

Dodds saw that the decision to retire brought huge relief to his platoon; there was even some standing up and mutual congratulations, as though they had risen from their seats and were collecting their belongings after a particularly riveting performance in the theater. They had to be brought back to order. Dodds thought sadly once more about what an unformidable group this small collection of decent men entrusted to him actually made in the aggregate. Always excepting Braddis—but where would they all be without Braddis? They were dutiful and unshirking and had mastered the basic skills expected of them as best they could. But mostly what they were, Dodds saw, was long-suffering. Several small men of poor physique from inadequate nutrition in their childhood were now accustomed to carrying loads too heavy for them on long, pointless marches without complaint. He had seen them in the baths, with their feet peeling, blistered, cracked, and rotting from standing guard in trenches for weeks in eight inches of water, and then the tearing itch of body lice and the pink and white leprous flesh of their inner thighs and underarms—crotch rot, as they called it—from the abrasions of dirty sodden serge uniforms, carefully marinated in a mixture of rain and sweat, a recipe yielding a balance of maddening itch and discomfort close to pain.

So now they would go home, back to their familiar trench. They should do it watchfully, Lieutenant Dodds emphasized, in single file at wide intervals. Private Alston would lead off with Section 3, covering their backs and directing their progress from point to point; they should move low to the ground all the way, and at each separate staging area they should lie down promptly and cover those coming on behind them. They should not move from any position until Private Alston gave the word. There was no rush: the point was to get everyone back safely—they had suffered too many casualties already.

Section 3 moved out without incident, and eventually turned a corner out of sight on the far side of a large mound excavated by a previous howitzer shell; Private Alston moved to join them. Sergeant Braddis, meanwhile, had been ranging from left to right behind him, Dodds noticed, and fired off two rounds at separate targets, before rejoining his section just in time to send it off. Dodds caught his eye and jerked his head in the direction of the shooting, by way of inquiry. Braddis nodded and joined him. "My practice over this stage of the game, sir, is to shoot at anything that moves. I've seen too many good men shot down in the home stretch by an enemy sniper or straggler looking for the last scalp of the day. All our men are accounted for, so anything moving out there, I assume, is not likely to be one of our well-wishers."

"Fair enough, Sergeant."

"A frustrating day's work, sir. I reckon we're lucky to be out of it at all, not that nine casualties out of thirty overall can be considered cheap."

"No. I think you're right on both counts." And the thought struck him that the letters he would have to write to the three dead men's families would bring his total to eleven, inside one year at the front.

Braddis had headed off to join his section, and Dodds's own men were now quietly filing one by one towards the safe haven of their mates in their own trench. Dodds himself was still lying facing out to the field covering Section 2's withdrawal, when he heard another shot coming from their direction, but, as he lay, off to the left. Probably Braddis again, but what enemy could be moving this close to their lines? He peered off in the direction of the shot, in case the person had been flushed out and was withdrawing towards him. Nothing. But it was time he rejoined his men anyway.

Braddis knew he was playing a game of narrow chances, but he was playing it under some compulsion, and he knew he had certain things going for him. Above all, he knew this passage of the terrain inch by inch in light or dark, and he had determined the exact point where he would make his move, if the chance was given. It had to be far enough out, and not on the doorstep of safety, to be plausible, and it would have to offer some blind cover back to his lines. His firing occasional shots off from here and there in the course of the withdrawal was designed to produce a kind of edginess to the proceedings, and break the rhythms; the men, he knew, would want to speed up and get back quicker to safety; and Dodds, he hoped, as he was responsible for covering for his men, might take some extra seconds to check that the area was, indeed, all clear. If you're watchful yourself, you can do a lot with a few moments of distraction. What he needed was a short gap separating Dodds from everyone but himself.

Braddis was a lucky man, as we know, and he got his gap. The place he had chosen was a curiously compact walled crater about fifty yards from the line, off to the side of the well-trodden path, offering a kind of private rampart, a hooked hiding place for a crouching man. Sure enough, Dodds came on, rifle at the ready, but moving faster than he normally would, trying to rejoin his section ahead. Braddis had a heavy German officer's pistol, a Luger—that treasured war-trophy of Allied soldiers—with its original ammunition; he had put it in his pack in the morning, and transferred it to the right-hand pocket of his fatigues in the pause before the order for withdrawal was given.

The moment Dodds passed, Braddis moved silently into the path behind him. His quarry was not more than six feet ahead— quite far enough for no powder burns to show on his uniform— and Braddis fired one shot from level ground, standing up. He considered it important that the trajectory of the bullet should not have an upward course, in case a medical officer was led to speculate that this was a round fired at very close quarters by an enemy in hiding just off the path. Braddis shot Dodds in the back, quite high up and to the left of the spine; the powerful, large-caliber bullet shattered the bone of the rib cage front and back, and tore out a piece of the heart on its passage through the chest. Braddis stepped aside and threw the gun into the standing water at the bottom of the crater, and fired his rifle off in no particular direction. He was with his man as he slowly crumpled and hit the ground on his back. Dodds was still conscious, but blood was pouring out of his chest, with a thin trickle also from the mouth.

Braddis raised him in his arms, and the young man stared up at him puzzled and trying to focus.

"I'm sorry, sir," Braddis said quietly. "You was shaping up to be a proper officer. But you see, sir, I couldn't run the risk of being put down again. That would have been intolerable to me."

"Braddis, I've left—" Dodds began to say, but the trickle from his mouth had grown to a flood, and he could not go on. He was finished.

Braddis stared at him, and then expertly frisked the body. He could not believe his luck. He pocketed what he had found, slung his rifle over his left shoulder, picked up his young platoon commander, and carried him back to his line.

CHAPTER 10

The Promise Canceled and Restored

MacIver knew he should concentrate on supper; he was not merely sick, but weak, and he had now fainted, if he remembered right, three times; and the fainting spells were starting to interfere with his writing. Furthermore, despite his fever, he was cold almost all the time, and he was now prepared to attribute a piece of that to his own lack of body fuel, and not merely the condition of the house. He had gone to bed last night in sweatshirt, sweatpants, two pairs of socks, and his vast navy greatcoat, precisely to stoke his fever into overdrive, so he could experience once more the increasingly rare sensation of actually being hot; and indeed, during the night he felt at least pleasantly warm—not quite the same as the wound-seeking, warmth-bestowing gift of Demerol, cocooning one's hurt into a heated and blessed oblivion, but certainly as good as one could expect at this stage of the game. So now it was on to supper, and here a touch of appetite had made its suggestion during the day, for what he had dubbed Sweet Gruel—the ancient secret MacIver clan recipe for toothless old men with blocked esophagi.

He had finally found a use for Margaret's mortar and pestle, those weighty and complementary stone utensils designed by Henry Moore, which he had found in a corner of the cupboard. To a base of lukewarm water (adjust temperature to taste), add three Pepperidge Farm lemon cookies, and mash them in the bowl to the smoothest paste. Swallowability is the key criterion of consistency. Add three heaped spoons of honey and as much single malt as your heart desires. Stir all together, and then spoon the concoction in small mouthfuls into the expectant gob. Follow each mouthful with a chaser of more warm water. MacIver followed the recipe assiduously and found it not at all bad. He even thought it aided the act of swallowing, which might well be due to the anesthetic effects of the Lagavulin— a point worth bearing in mind for future applications. He was so pleased with his patented concoction that he repeated it on four successive nights, until he found that the packet of cookies was empty. So after that he narrowed the recipe to Lagavulin and warm maple syrup. He was not at all sure he didn't prefer it in this simpler version. But Lagavulin with maple syrup! My God, how sick he must be.

After supper it was back to the rocking chair, with Beethoven's lovely late quartet, opus 132, and the slow movement that he called "A reverent song of thanks from an invalid made well"—the gentle laying down of large, sonorous chords, safe, weighty, well-spaced stepping-stones that lead you up and down but which will eventually rise inexorably, one on top of the other, on and on, up and up, to the most insistent climax. It is all gravely paced to the recovered invalid's discovery that at last he can rise from bed and walk confidently again. MacIver and Margaret had always thought it justified its title perfectly— it breathes out not only consolation, but a sense of having been consoled. MacIver wondered now whether Beethoven had known at the time that he was not actually fully recovered, though he had almost two years to live (an eternity, of course, compared with the brief number of days being counted in the Night Heron House). He did not live well in those two years, persecuting his nephew Karl in the most predatory way. But the force of the hymn acknowledges that we all achieve a touch of innocence in our simple gratitude for any alleviation of our condition.

The death of David had been the worst thing that had ever happened to either of them, and well over half of the year that followed it (MacIver was ashamed to remember just how bad and for how long) was certainly the worst extended period either of them had lived through. He knew that if blame was ever fairly apportioned for their fall from grace and ease with each other, most of it must come to him. If David were to appear sitting opposite him and listening to the music, he would tell him gently but firmly that he had nearly lost for all time the greatest blessing he was ever given.

The trouble had started as soon as they came back from the funeral at Arlington. In fact he had started an argument about that before they went: why would they put their private grief in the context of the great national charade, the flags, the rifle shots, the bugle calls, which in another, seamier, context—one they strongly disapproved of—had demanded their son's life? But Margaret had said they had to go: "These are the people David chose to live among, and this is the way they pay their respect to a fallen comrade and friend. David wouldn't reject their kindness and nor should we. And Stafford Dionne has said he will be there, and I wouldn't do anything to hurt that boy for the world."

And, of course, as always Margaret had read it right. Stafford was there, and in fact commanded the honor guard, and brought to Margaret at the end the swiftly, neatly folded triangle of flag. There is probably a well-worded message that the soldier speaks on these occasions, but Stafford with tremulous voice said simply, "Mr. and Mrs. MacIver, this comes to you with the love and thanks of David's friends, and the greatest sorrow for your loss." It was all he had to give. And Margaret with eyes brimming but voice composed said: "Thank you, Stafford. We will fly it at our house at the Cape, and think of David and you and all your friends. You must come and see us." And he, fighting his emotions but returning to script, had saluted and rejoined his unit. They had flown the flag briefly, before they started falling.

The problem was that grief carried the two of them in orthogonal directions, apart. But a harsher view would say that it was the indiscriminate, omnivorous rage of MacIver that was sundering them. It flashed, apparently out of quiet, onto all and sundry, including people for whom normally he showed great respect—handymen, craftsmen working on the house—and even his students. One day, in the first-year humanities class that he always insisted on teaching, he found, as is often the case in the class after a midterm, the section sluggish in its interest and vague in the details of the text of the day, which happened to be *Lear*. After yet another question fell silently to the ground unanswered—where would you say the first moment in this play occurs, when Lear is interested in anything but himself?—he stared out balefully at the class, letting the silence thicken around them all to induce discomfort, and then quietly but witheringly raked them with his rage:

"Allow yourselves to feel something, you smug little spastics. Or at least concentrate to the point that you may stumble over some disturbing passage or fact, which, considered in the small hours over the years, may finally agitate you into being a little more human."

At which a good student, with dignity and some hurt, asked quietly: "Why are you so angry at us, sir?"

The malignant energy, operating willfully to alienate them, immediately drained away, and MacIver said wearily, "Oh, I don't know. I'm very sorry. Personal disappointment, perhaps." (He would never call it grief, but his desolation must have been obvious to them.) "But I hope that it's a little larger than that. There seems such a disproportion between what actually happens in the world, and keeps on happening, and the way we talk about it, and have always talked about it, *here*—in this sort of setting. We just, contentedly for the most part, lay words on things, and let them lie."

The dean, who liked him, and whom MacIver admired, heard about some of these exchanges and suggested they have lunch. They went downtown, to be anonymous and uninterrupted.

"I hear things, Robert," the dean began, sipping his merlot appraisingly, "that go beyond MacIver impatience and irritation to something heavier. Shall I recite?"

"No need," said MacIver. "They're true. They happened. I'm not good at controlling them right now."

"You've never really got the hang of the academy—you're a little too large and raw-boned for it. You make people nervous. For your average academic the institution serves as a tepid bath of ease and discontent. Out of the discontent sometimes comes a little ferment, which is brought to focus, and lo! an original piece of science or scholarship pops out. Then over the hill, blotting out the sun, comes stomping your heavy Highland Prophet, full of denunciations and roiling of waters, flipping a couple of little sharks from his bucket into the bath. You can see how gentle people might find this unnerving rather than bracing?"

"I've always admired how, in your narration of a situation, you always cling to the strictly factual."

"Even a dean has to keep himself amused, Robert."

"Are you suggesting that I should give up history, and go into, say, road construction?"

"There you go. Perfect. You can line up all your enemies in the sticky tar, and then run them over with your steamroller; in fact, while you're at it I'll send you a couple of dozen of mine. No, I'm suggesting that you take a leave of absence next term. It's all right"—holding up his hand to stop MacIver's interruption—"I can fund it for you—so that you and Margaret can help each other come through this awful thing that has befallen you. As it is, you're frayed too thin, and it looks to me as though you're in danger of coming apart."

"It may be too late," said MacIver. "I've been impossible at home, and I think I may be driving her away from me."

"That would be the saddest thing I've heard yet," said the dean, and MacIver could see he meant it. "In the meantime," he went on, "there are only nine classes left in the term, and you have to keep the lid on through those. I have always wanted our students to be taught by your passion, but they can't be shredded in the process. They're not to be treated as though they were some sort of scabs; we actually don't want them to be in Vietnam, right? We want to keep them safe right here. Remember the students you gave a charge to—Katherine Corton, Phil Ogden, dozens of them. That's the way to go: spark them, don't scorch them. Make it so."

"You're a good friend to me, Andrew."

"Ah, well. We bloody-minded men should stick together."

At home on Riverside Drive, the situation was as bad as MacIver had described, and he knew he made it so. He would go to his office in Fayerweather and sit there most of the day, idly turning pages and penciling spidery notes on a legal pad, a few usually caustic words, trailing behind a row of dots into inconsequence. The youthful verve with which he had assembled a coherent argument in the past was gone—the piles of books with pencils stuck at the relevant page with the telltale quotes detailing the most flagrant examples of Schnorkelbaum's error on this side, reams of articles with savage double tracks of marker-pen down the side of the page showing Fitz-Fotheringay's most absurd overstatements over there, while down the middle, in a blaze of humane moderation, went sailing the Scottish center MacIver cutting through another overextended line to another luminous score.

All that was over. His colleagues were compassionate, mostly, and for a while tried to divert him from his grief by inviting him to do this or that manageable piece of work—contribute to a Festschrift for this retiring scholar, give a short address at the principal conference on oral history, join a group planning a new sequence of electives for majors—but he rejected everything, and usually churlishly: the scholar was a mountain of pedantry, the conference had long ago fallen into the hands of the self-promoting brainless, and the proposed sequence of courses had no internal rhyme or reason, amounting to no more than a smug parade of political certainties. He made it clear that he wanted to be left alone, so they left him alone.

Back at the house, waiting for Margaret to get back from the studio she had taken downtown, he made himself tea, and stood looking out at the gaunt tree branches of Riverside Park, seeing the seams and grooves of the bark absorbed into stark, black silhouettes as the afternoon wore down. He knew he had stated the matter accurately to the dean: Margaret might well be taking a leave of absence of her own; he could feel it coming, and could not blame her for it, and didn't seem able to take steps to stop it. He stood there pondering this state of total aporia. One step farther out from their high windows, the great river still caught the light, with plates and lozenges of ice herded into a side stream by the current and the tide, welded here and there into barriers to enclose a glassy lagoon away from the chop of the stream. Margaret found him still looking down there when the thin horizontal clouds over the Palisades had been turned into angry red splinters by the sunset.

"Any great battles, rejections, put-downs, or altercations today?" she asked, looking at him, he knew, dispassionately and seeing a man in deep despair.

"Not today. Today a quiet one of harboring diminishing resources for future frays. You know, the cruel thing about depression is not that it makes you see the world darkly; God knows at my jauntiest, I've always looked on the world darkly. How else should one look at the bloody thing? The real debasing role of depression is to remove all flashes of energy or concentration, to ensure that you can never complete anything. Depression as depth fatigue. It takes a particular zest in grinding you to immobility, so that you have no smidgeon of self-esteem left. It's my kind of guy—no half-measures, takes no prisoners."

"Yes, I think that sounds true. How did your lunch with Andrew go?"

"It was good. He's such an unusual mix—a picture of wry disengagement, and a kind of effortless caring to do the right thing at the same time. He wants me to take a leave of absence next term, to stop strafing all and sundry and leave the university some wholesome happiness—he will pay for it."

"He's such a nice man. What do you think of that?"

"I'm inclined to do it. As long as I keep going through the same motions, they seem imprisoning to me; they've already proved to me that they can't sustain me in my present state, so they have become incrementally demoralizing. I need to go through some different motions, and I'm going to look for a pill dispenser."

"Really?" She was surprised.

"Yes. Do you think Andrew dispenses pills? The trouble is I don't want to do too much talking to get pills. I don't want to sit around analyzing why my father went up in the air, so he wouldn't come down in the mud, and the terrible stain it left on me."

"No, I know you wouldn't want to do too much of that. Even if Andrew doesn't dispense himself, I'm sure he would know someone who does. And he could always convey to the person that, in your present state of mind, the therapist will not want to be in the same room with you for any longer than it takes to write a prescription."

"Shall I take you out to dinner so that we can talk more about this and us? The food won't be as good as you make, but we can think of somewhere quiet and private, and settle in."

"What a great idea! What about going back to Anita and Jen's? They're better than I am, and they keep a lovely quiet place."

So they went and ate and drank well and talked till they were alone in the restaurant. MacIver liked premises stated in advance in this sort of discussion, which always amused Margaret—it seems a male prerequisite to state the obvious, as though needing to clear the ground first of the very few propositions you won't get around to fighting over.

"We know each other very well, and we've never lied to each other. All my motions seem rutted here, and I can't get out of them. I think we both need to take some time away from each other, because of the bad way I keep hounding you with my intemperate rage. I don't know how long it's going to take me to bring myself to heel, and I need to bring myself up short, to confront the grimness of life without you."

"Are you sure I'm not one of the motions you want to get away from?"

"Entirely sure. You're the one motion and rhythm I want and need to get back to, and every day I tell myself that, and every day the Black Dog, the Black Bile, whatever, takes me by the throat and twists my every intention to the ugly outburst. I need to hear from you right now just how bad it's been."

"It's been bad. I won't deny it. And at its worst I've wondered whether I am finally seeing your true nature. From the time we met at Sally's gallery until David's death we were all pleasure-loving people. David loved almost every minute of living till the end, and if he were still alive he would still be loving it, even without a leg. And I intend to go on trying to find pleasure in my life; but you seem to recoil from the very notion of pleasure, even when you might find some relief in it; it's as though you've got some grim, bile-laden gene, preaching to you in a rasping voice that to find pleasure is to betray memory."

"My poor love. Harsh but fair."

"The other thing is your famous anger. I get angry myself. You know, I had a son, and I lost him, too. Remember? And sometimes I am literally sick with anger. But I don't use it as a flail on other people."

"And I use mine that way?"

"Look at it and see. Do you get a cheap thrill out of it? (Not pleasure, of course.) You're articulate and you're quick, and the worst of you, I believe, rather likes blowing people away. If I'm right, along with your decency there's a bit of a bully left in you, and it's a rotten thing. And it's destructive, too, not just to the people you hurt, but to yourself. It's as though you torch the whole landscape with your flamethrower, and then when you finally look at what you've done, you find it ugly—MacIver's handmade Menin Road. So it's self-perpetuating: the anger at the ugliness of what you've made makes you angry again."

"Why did you wait till now to say this?"

"Oh, for God's sake. I've tried to talk to you about it before, but you weren't ever receptive to hearing it—it got the distracted brush-off line, 'Yeah, right—I know' or 'Yes, I keep trying to turn it off, but I can't right now.' "

"Yes, I'm sorry again, I can remember more than a couple of those. I'm hearing it now."

"So what do we do?"

"What do you think of this idea that we spend a short time apart—in touch, but apart? I've hurt you, and seen you withdraw from me, and I have to stop that or lose you. I was hoping we would spend the summer together as usual, and I would get medication, to kick the psyche into a better frame of mind, and get myself in better physical shape, and work hard on the house. I would tell Andrew that I'd like to take him up on his offer of a leave, so I wouldn't be at Columbia in the first semester and ready to slip easily back into the recent pattern of clobbering students and colleagues. Instead I was thinking of taking up the offer of my old friends in Edinburgh, and spending a term there. And I wouldn't go till the end of September, because they don't start till later, and finish in early December. The brainy Brits have a good idea there—keep actual school time to a minimum. So we would be back together by Christmas, and hopefully I could give you a brand-new mint MacIver as one of my presents. I'm also thinking I might start a new research interest— moving on a war. I want to study Lord Lovat and his first regiment of commandos in World War Two. Most of them were his tenants, gillies and crofters off the Fraser estates, all clansmen of his. I would talk to them—what the war was like, but more on what it was like to be plucked out of the highlands in the first place, and what it was like to be going back there, after seeing Paris etcetera. Most of them would be in their late forties, early fifties, so there should be plenty of them around with their stories. The question is, what do you think of the plan, and where would you be?"

She watched his face with pleasure, seeing some life in the eyes and animation for the first time, she thought, since October. "I love the new research project, but the thought of a mint MacIver is a little alarming. What if I don't like it? Like a new, sassy car model, where you can never find what opens the flap to the gas tank, and the windshield-wiper switch turns up the stereo speakers in the back. I like my old battered MacIver model, for all its rattles and engine noise, its gas guzzling and rusting tailpipe." She gave her soft, merry laugh—she loved to score on him.

"Thank you," he said. "Let's not take that any further. The question is, what would you be doing with yourself?"

"Aha! By a curious chance, this very day I have been offered the perfect Andrew analogue."

And it turned out that Karl Ferenyi, a graceful and civilized old collector, who admired Margaret, and for a long time had urged her to do illustrations for handsome volumes he would produce, had finally hit on one she was prepared to consider— a lavishly printed and bound edition of *Paradise Lost*, to be made in Paris, on almost as opulent a scale as William Morris's *Chaucer*. It would be a long extension on what she had been doing, but her present grief made the large, dark theme attractive. Twelve original plates in the volume, one for each book of the poem, and she could pick the text or theme of each plate for herself, making her own match to particular passages that caught her eye. The terms would be generous.

Margaret was now eager to do this. She knew Milton, and she knew Blake on Milton, and though she wondered whether her reverence for both of them might inhibit her, she had already picked her theme and an emphasis within the theme, which would give the hint of coherence to the twelve plates on their separate pages. She would paint falling figures, and the emphasis common to all of them would be that the bodies must have weight, be subject to gravity, and not simply ethereal spirits, because they were all sinners. She had already chosen the text for her first plate: *Him the Almighty Power / Hurl'd headlong flaming from th' Ethereal Sky / With Hideous Ruin. 1:44–46.* "I've been thinking about it all day," she said. "And the phrase that keeps turning in my mind is the phrase *free fall*—I think it's almost an oxymoron. The only free fall I have ever seen is that of trapeze artists, when, weary after their nerve- and muscle-burning stunts on the swinging bar and the split-second catches in the bright lights, they can suddenly let themselves go and drop down loose and free into the safety net below, on their way back to earth. But most falls aren't free—there is always the tension, it seems to me, between what you are falling from and what you are falling to."

MacIver listened to her, admiring and envying once more the richness of his wife's inner life, the way her experience, however traumatic, seemed to flow, almost at once, always naturally into streams of creative impulse in the center of her, and color them. He told her.

So the evening where they spelled things out together turned brighter at this decision that they would be the better part of three months apart, but the distance between them would be only the one hour and fifteen minutes on British Caledonian, from Edinburgh to Paris.

"And what are the rules on visitation?" he asked.

"Oh, surely three weekends. We can handle that, even if you're still an ogre, and we can't get by with fewer."

"Are we playing them on a home and away basis?"

"No, we're playing the first one in Edinburgh in October, and the other two in Paris. I can't be in Scotland in the cold."

"What about sex? Are we committed to monk and nun?"

"Monk and nun except on visitation weekends, when we become Abelard and Héloïse."

"How will you handle the ancient, insinuating Ferenyi?"

"Unlike some other people, Karl is content with other parts of me than my body."

"The swine."

They talked on. How would they spend their time, when they weren't talking to commandos or painting Milton? MacIver confided a little sheepishly that he might volunteer to help coach the rugby team at Heriot's. "They make a lot of me there."

"Do they ever," she said, feigning indignation. "It was obscene how they fawned over you there when you took me back after we were married. But you are an utter, utter cad. I had been flattering myself that you wanted to get back in shape to appeal to your poor wife, and it turns out you just want to strut in front of teenage boys. . . ."

"Not strut, but at least to trot down the field, if I can't sprint down it. What are you going to be doing all fancy-free in Paris in your loose hours?"

"I may have to work harder than I like. I've never illustrated a book before, let alone such a luxurious volume. And I've never collaborated with a team of people before. I always liked the solitude of being an artist. But now I'll have to learn new things, but that's all right because I'm in the mood for some company. Otherwise, I'll do what one always does in Paris, I'll pick up shiny chestnuts in the Place des Vosges and watch children float ancient wooden toy boats with faded sails in the ponds of the Tuileries gardens and sit in cafés and sip what the mood of the moment orders and drink in everything else, and go to concerts in churches in the evening, and read. And occasionally I'll think of you."

They went home easier than they had been since October, and the next day, without prodding, MacIver phoned the well-connected dean to see if he had any recommendation for a therapist.

"Ah, yes," said Andrew. "Excellent. Do you want a man or a woman? Be very careful what you answer."

"I'll leave it entirely to you. But you do understand that I want the person who lets me leave with the fewest words spoken, but holding in my big mitt an illegible prescription scrawled on white paper, which will however lead directly to some Merlin elixir which restores me to myself and general happiness in a matter of days."

"I understand everything perfectly," said the dean, playing with his smooth shrink's voice. The trouble with Andrew is that he does, thought MacIver. He's really very irritating.

Irritating or not, the next morning he sent in the phone number of a woman, whom MacIver called at once, and found to be pleasant voiced, matter-of-fact, and with several slots available in her schedule over the next few days. He took the first one, and a youngish woman, late thirties he calculated, greeted him at the scheduled hour and took him into a light, sparely but elegantly furnished room with some nice drawings and small paintings, which he would have liked to explore.

"I don't know what Dean Repton told you about me," he began.

"He told me that you and your wife had lost a wonderful son in Vietnam in October, that things had been very hard for you since then, that you had, to use his words, one of the great marriages of our time, and the two of you are about to go abroad. So where I can help you best right now, it seems to me, is to give you something that helps ease the burden; it won't change any of the facts, but it may have the effect of letting a little more light in, so you can attend to other things besides the sorrow itself. I gather that we may have a little time to get the dose right before you go off, and then I could send you on your way with enough medication to hold you through Christmas. But it will help if you tell me exactly what your symptoms have been over these last few months."

So MacIver told her, and well, with sharply focused vignettes of each kind of lost control—the sudden flash-fury to hapless students, the listless unyielding wall of moroseness rebuffing Margaret's loving efforts to reach him, the extraordinary depth of fatigue pulling him back to bed at eleven after he had slept from ten at night to nine in the morning, the complete desertion of any powers of concentration, forcing him to write out a sentence in a book in the hope that slowing the attention to each laborious letter might bring understanding of the whole thought, and finally the continually haunting final picture, crowding back unbidden at every hour, of his son in the hospital morgue. He told it all in an even voice, with pauses. "I don't know if any of that helps," he said. "My wife Margaret could tell you a lot more."

"That is quite enough for what I need," the young doctor said quietly. As he was on his way to the door with his prescription, she added an afterthought: "I actually know you both from your work."

"Ah! How so?" he said.

"In college my history professor had us all read *Voices Through the Smoke* for our course on the twentieth century, 'Death of Victoria to Victory over Japan.'" She was both charmingly embarrassed and amused at herself at the same time. "He said, I remember, it was the first book of history to display the horrors of war extended indefinitely forward in individual lives with the sustained force of a poetic image."

"Did he now? I think Thucydides may have got there first, but it is in fact exactly what I tried to do. How nice of you to mention it to me. But how do you know Margaret?"

"Oh, I own a Margaret Westleigh! It used to hang right there on the wall, but I liked it so much I had to have it at home."

"Can I ask what it's a picture of?"

"Yes, of course. It's one of her softly lit interiors, with the viewer looking in from outside, and there's a young woman, whom you see in profile, with her hand half-extended, clearly deliberating whether to pick up a photograph on the table in front of her."

"I remember that picture!" MacIver exclaimed. "It was hanging in her show at the Gordon Gallery in 1947 on the day I met her for the first time. It tells a story, doesn't it, but you're never quite sure what it is. You have to assume, though, that the young woman is not in her own room."

"Exactly," she laughed. "But is she in her lover's room looking at a photograph of him and his wife, or in her father's room, and the photograph's of him and an unknown woman, not her mother? And so on. I can speculate for the rest of my life!"

They parted with pleasure at having met, but as soon as he closed the office door, he hastened across Fifth Avenue and sat on a bench with his back to the Park, and tears welled up within him from the telling. "That's what I was afraid of," he scolded himself. "Perhaps we've all got some Ben Winterbourne in us."

However, the dinner downtown and this visit to Dr. Ehrlich were a turning point for both of them, sending them on the way back together. They had a very productive summer on the Cape, with Margaret completing no fewer than five of her Milton paintings, and sketches of another four, and MacIver working very hard at getting fit, cycling miles every morning, running every evening on Newcomb's Hollow beach after the crowds had left, and during the day cutting cords of wood at the chopping block, swinging like an executioner. Margaret could observe him from the window: "You're getting much more accurate," she remarked. "Before, I used to worry about your feet, but now you could split a match lengthwise."

Their European adventure was everything they could have wished. Ferenyi had taken a beautiful studio for Margaret on the Ile Saint-Louis, overlooking the Seine, and MacIver had sublet the flat of P. G. Walsh, a good classicist on leave, high up on Castle Hill looking out to Holyrood. They kept to their visitation schedule, both craving for the calendar to move faster after each visit was ended. Edinburgh disarmed itself for the first one into one of its splendid autumnal moods of mellow gold; Paris was always Paris. As they had in their first beginnings before they were married, in both places they left rumpled sheets behind, and turned gentle faces to each other as they went about their short days.

Work went well, too. Ferenyi was ecstatic with Margaret's Milton paintings, and, to his delight, she got heavily involved in the process of design of the whole book. Territorial jealousies between the great craftsmen he had enlisted were largely hushed in her presence; she saw the best in each person's work, and she saw ways to make the best combine to make them all look better.

MacIver immediately got caught up with his commandos; these were not broken men, like the victims of the gas attacks. They had seen much more of war than he ever had, and much worse things. Most of them seemed to him, as they met in each soldier's pub of choice over beer or whisky, to possess a kind of quiet containment; they all had in their bones the often splendid, often desolate rhythms of burn, loch, glen, and moor. Some had gone back to old estates and stayed, most had not. Whatever had been thrown at them in their lives, they had more than managed. To his surprise their largest concerns seemed mostly for their children, who had far fewer assurances in their modern lives than Lovat's men and their wives had brought from their almost feudal childhoods.

He gave two afternoons a week to Heriot's rugby First Fifteen. Their regular coach, Glen Duncan, an enormous second-row forward, who in his day had also played for Scotland, had hugged the air out of him and said, "This is what we need. You do the backs, and I'll do the forwards. The little fuckers will die for you." So the old Ginger Fox dusted off some of his ancient guiles and throughly enjoyed himself. He taught them how to study the man marking them for a weakness ("He may well tackle better to one side than the other, preferring to lead with his right shoulder, say, so you'll know which way to cut on him"); the small tough scrum-half Kevin reminded him of his friend Terry, but he needed more strings to his bow. ("You've got a lovely long serve from the bottom of the scrum, but if you use it all the time, you just keep showing the wing-forward where his target is going to get the ball; we need to work with you and Gary on getting some variety in there. Don't forget the blind side.") He had never known a team more eager to learn, both with the ball and defending. Once, feeling particularly frisky at practice, he took his place in the line as they passed down the field, with just the faintest hint of his old bullish stride and even side-step, but Coach Duncan had caught a glimpse from an adjacent practice field, and started chanting Mac-I-ver! Mac-I-ver! and the rest of the team stopped whatever it was doing and loudly joined in, so he had had to flick the ball to the young center next to him, before he tore something and died of humiliation.

The long weekend of Margaret's visit to Edinburgh coincided with the first anniversary of David's death. The actual anniversary was a Friday, but they had talked about it, and both of them wanted to spend the day together, so she had come on Thursday morning. For the Friday, MacIver had rented a car for the day, and they drove out to the north of the city—to Kinross on Loch Leven, where Mary Queen of Scots had been kept prisoner, but escaped. Then they had gone on through Falkland to Perth, where as a boy he had ridden horses on the hills above the Tay estuary. They looked quietly at what there was to see on that golden October day, and they talked.

"I know it's irrational, but I'm like a child who believes he was given a treasure, and feels guilty for losing it," he said.

Margaret kept urging him past this mis-feeling, rather than misreading, of the situation. "I felt some of that, too," she said, "but I have convinced myself that it's just a symptom of real loss; there *is* an 'ought' in the situation—he really ought to be here, but the fact that he's not is not our fault: it was never in our hands. But one sure thing is that David would want us to enjoy these weekends, and not mope over him. So starting tomorrow you must show me your new Edinburgh." As always, she kept trying to lead him back to better spirits. They parked the car and walked and kept talking, though there were comfortable silences too. And now when he looked at her, he began to see what loss had done.

On the last hill of the day, as they looked down at the pale ribbon of the Tay below them dissolving itself into the Indian summer haze over the North Sea, he studied her face and with a little shock finally realized that she was lonely. He put his arm around her shoulder and turned her to face him, and said: "He was more you than me, more yours than mine, and for all his life I never resented it for a moment, but gloried in it—it was as though there was more of both of you to love. But the instant he died, something vile in me started grabbing to get all of him. And I lost myself and you. It's the worst thing I've done, and I've never said I'm sorry for doing it. But I'm saying it now." She hugged him and wept.

That night they made love again very gently, and Margaret touched his rough face with wondering fingers, moving lightly over all his features as though trying to make what had become strange feel familiar again. When she drifted off to sleep curled against him, he suddenly recalled a visit he had made to her studio in the house about a month after David had died. She never minded his watching her paint, but he knew better than to start a conversation while she was engaged. On the easel was a new painting: a ruined Celtic chapel on a headland—it could almost have been above the Tay that afternoon—with an overgrown garden or cemetery, a high wall in partial collapse, and what was left grappled with a tumble of weed and ivy. On the seaward side there was a derelict doorway with its lintel still intact, and over it was an inscription from Isaiah, still legible in the weathered stone: "Fear not: for I have redeemed thee, I have called thee by thy name; thou art mine. When thou passest through the waters, I shall be with thee; and through the rivers, they shall not overflow thee. . . ." Lovely words, but the view through the doorway down to the sea was chillingly bleak. The color chosen for the water was the darkest grey, one halftone from black. MacIver knew she had never before done anything so desolate. But it wasn't finished.

In the foreground, almost at the observer's feet, was a new grave, with an engraved stone but without a name or dates. The soil around it had been recently cleared, an inscription freshly limned on the clean granite, no lichen or meandering cracks. But when he read the inscription he recognized at once that the words were taken from one of David's letters. This was his grave.

Soon after he had started his helicopter duty, carrying the wounded from battlefield to field hospital, he had written a long letter, first describing the novel sensation of being in the machine, but then moving his focus to the impact on the landscape and the people who work it. ". . . A helicopter in the middle distance is just a nondescript mosquito with a drone, but as it approaches, different levels of noise start asserting themselves; the woofer of the rotary kicks in (BA-BA-BA-BA) and becomes ever louder, and when you fly low (which we usually do, because it is harder for anyone on the ground to draw a bead on us at that pace), you are inscribing an earsplitting incision of noise on the fields you are rushing over, often only twenty-five feet below. They have been harvesting the rice from the swampy paddies over the last couple of weeks, lines of figures bent to the work, a curve of mostly white clothes under the fine yellow conical hats, held in a permanent stoop over the individual plants. They don't look up anymore when we pass; my pilot says when he started out here they would sometimes stand up, and occasionally even wave, but not now. I've noticed a few children down there, but they don't look up either. They are working their land, doing what their grandparents did, and it is their place. With our constant rush and constant noise pressing down on them, I cannot avoid the *invasiveness* of what we do. Everyone needs a place, and this is not ours. I have been wondering where mine is. Not New York, not Wellfleet. You, I now know, are mine. . . ."

Margaret had edited the ending, and blocked out space on her granite stone, and penciled lettering for it to read:

EVERYONE NEEDS A PLACE, AND THIS IS NOT OURS.
I WONDER WHERE IS MINE? NOWHERE I CAN NAME.
YOU, I NOW KNOW, ARE MINE.

But she could not paint the words. She was staring in misery at this bottom corner of her painting, and MacIver could see David's letter, much creased from being read, reread, memorized, on the table beside her. "It won't work," she said. "He never wrote the words for a stone or a painting. . . . The new won't fit with the old here. . . . It will always be apart." And now she was weeping, and MacIver held her and felt her shuddering sobs into his body, as he had that awful morning at the hospital. "How could you have ignored all this?" he asked himself, and turned now to hold her in her sleep.

If MacIver's world started to open up again with a view into his wife's grief, the next day it expanded further by seeing deeper into her buoyancy. Before the weekend he had sent her in Paris a list of Edinburgh's coming events, so they could plan their activities—there was an exhibition of late-nineteenth-century Scottish painting at the National Gallery of Scotland, which included three women painters she was interested in, and there was a good concert at Usher Hall. "There's just one fly in the ointment," he had written. "Saturday afternoon is Heriot's big match against its hated rival. As coach for half the team, I reckon I should put in an appearance, but only for half the game. It will take me an hour and ten minutes going and coming, to rejoin you at whatever you choose to be doing." But on the Saturday morning she said she wanted to come with him to the game, "if that's all right. I never saw you play, so I'd like to see the boys you coach."

So on the Saturday afternoon, he had taken her down to the second half. They stood on the sideline in the big, noisy throng, and MacIver stationed her in front of him, with his hands on her shoulders, or in a relaxed moment enfolding her: he was swiftly into the game, roaring over her head "Up on him, Colin!" when the enemy had the ball, or muttering "Oh for God's sake" when Heriot's dropped it. She could feel herself catching his excitement through the tension in his body. They had arrived with the score tied 6–6, but then with time short Duncan's forwards had started grinding with precision down the field against a tired and outweighed pack, with the fly-half Gary gaining yards with some elegant kicking for touch. Margaret was by now shouting with the crowd. Heriot's finally forced a five-yard scrum near the enemy line, and MacIver's pupil Kevin got the ball, feinted his usual pass to Gary, but instead did a lovely reverse pass to the blind side, where their speedy winger, like a fair-haired, diving dart, took the ball in full stride and shot over for the try. Total bedlam—maybe better than beating England. Margaret turned, looked up at him beaming, and said, "You taught them well!" The final whistle blew and MacIver took her hand, and they trotted out onto the field to join the team celebrating around their coach. In his exuberance, Duncan, who had never met Margaret before, picked her up by her elbows, raised her to his full six-eight, and kissed her resoundingly on both cheeks, before setting her gently down again. She was still breathless at supper that night: "That coach is a *giant*," she said, looking at MacIver across the table, her eyes round with wonder.

It was in the evenings, of course, that he missed her most and felt small prickings of jealousy against her admirer Ferenyi, who saw so much more of her than he did. The thought occurred to him: why should he not also commission some works of art from her? So sitting at his borrowed desk one night, after sorting through the notes he had taken in his interviews that day, he decided to embark on a children's story, and sketched out its title page:

The Cat Who Knew His Mind
STUDIES OF OPINIONATED ANIMALS, VOL. I

by

Robert D. MacIver, B.A., M.A. Oxon,
Ph.D. Columbia, D.Litt. Edinburgh, etc.

On page 2, the story began:

"We are all very lucky to live in a well-ordered household," said Bluto, the bloodhound, to the other three dogs and the cat. He considered himself their leader, not only because of his size, but because of his unique social skill of absorbing three (3) tennis balls into his soft, leathery jowls at once, rotating them there for a while, and then disgorging them on the rug with their yellow covers all pulpy and disgusting strands of saliva draped over them.

"Bullshit," said Lord Stripington, reclining in his usual place on the bookshelf in front of the works of Hobbes. "In a well-ordered house, dogs who roll in manure outside would not be allowed inside. . . ."

The story drifted on to its moralistic conclusion, and the triumph of Lord Stripington and the border collie Kipper, who becomes his buddy. MacIver had singled out the passages he required for illustration:

1. "For a fellow who lies around in his striped pyjamas all day, he's really an efficient little killer," said the border collie admiringly.
2. "Just shin up the tree, Stripy old boy, and tell us if you see anyone coming," said Kipper to his friend.

MacIver phoned Margaret and said some important materials were on their way, and within a week received the two illustrations back, much better than their text deserved, and a third, with a truly adorable, small, clearly feminine cat saying to Lord Stripington, looking as supercilious as the New York Public Library lions: "Lord Stripington, do you think a worldly, knowledgeable fellow like you would soon get bored with a diffident girl like me?" It was the first they had played together, MacIver calculated, since David had come home from Yale.

MacIver went skipping over to Paris as soon as the term was over in early December, and they celebrated their twenty-fourth wedding anniversary in style on Christmas Eve. After a walk along the cliff's thin edge, they were back together again.

CHAPTER 11

No Glorious End for Warriors

Sergeant Braddis was not ready for the horror that greeted him when he returned to the line carrying Dodds's body, the limp figure's uniform crimsoned from neck to knee, the face pale as wax under the soft brown hair, the whole head lolling back and to the right, as though it had had its throat cut, Braddis himself breathing heavily and sweating, fatigues almost as dyed with the young man's blood as his victim. Hands were raised to take the body and lay him out on a groundsheet spread along the fire-step. No one was looking at the sergeant, who stood a little off to the side, telling what happened.

"I'm just making it back to my section, and ready for the last lap home, and suddenly there's a shot behind me, and I go running back. I'd been worried all the way during our withdrawal; I'd seen a skulker between mounds, just a shoulder disappearing as I turned sort of thing, and fired off a couple of rounds at him, hoping to chase him off. But he clearly wasn't going home till he'd had a clean shot, and taken someone out. Maybe he just wanted the officer, knowing that he would be covering the rear of the platoon. Anyway, I get there just as Mr. Dodds is crumpling, so I half-catch him and am holding him and he's got blood pouring from the chest, but it's an exit wound, I could tell, so he was shot in the back; and he's got more blood coming out of his mouth, but he looks up and says 'Thank you, Sergeant' rather faint, and then he can't talk anymore, and he's gone. Always a gentleman, Mr. Dodds."

They were hearing him, not looking at him, as though they were ashamed for him. He felt like smacking them to attention, with a firm "Do you understand what I'm telling you?" dressing them down like a sergeant, but the thought occurred to him that he was in charge of the platoon now, and should try playing it in a quieter way, like an officer. Who knows, he might even get a commission out of this: the beautiful thing about war was that officers often have their hand forced to do things that would never occur to them in peace. Other NCOs had got their Sam Browne belt and the King's letter in these situations, and, after all, Braddis knew he was the best man they had. The one diffidence at his core was that he would never know how many of the men believed him.

Indeed, the fatal flaw in Braddis was that he never cared, and therefore never knew, what other people were thinking. It had never occurred to him that Lieutenant Dodds was well liked and respected by the platoon. The animal schooled for predation on instinct had scant room for moral judgment. For him, general rules of right or wrong stopped pretty much with parade-ground etiquette. Beyond those geometrically ordered bounds, especially out on the battlefield, he made his own rules, and they had been quite successful for him. The quieter shadings of good into decent were nonexistent for him. The thought that other people might have feelings on such things, and strong feelings, and even act on them, and that indeed society was sometimes organized to pay deference to such feelings, was wasted on him. His neglect of such niceties was what had caused his demotion to sergeant for raiding the quartermaster stores at Caterham, and what he had done in no-man's-land this afternoon would be ruinous for him, as it should be. But before another twenty-four hours were out he would have curiously compounded his predicament because of exactly the same neglect.

Simon Dodds had written a memo to the company adjutant, Captain Alan Leslie, about Braddis. His batman, a small, shy, punctilious man who revered his officer, had delivered it to company HQ that morning, and as Dodds had omitted any dramatic note on the envelope, such as "Open in the event of death," Leslie had read it straightaway. It's not clear whether Dodds was simply passing on the worrying question of Braddis's looting to a more seasoned and experienced officer (Leslie was in his forties, a good Yorkshireman with an established practice as a solicitor in Whitby), or whether Dodds had some premonition that Braddis might resort to violence to stop just such a memo as this letter. Leslie knew all about Braddis, and the letter disturbed him when he read it. He regarded young Dodds as a friend—the two of them had had some happy escapist conversations in the officers' mess about their mutual passion for sailing. When the news came of his death, brought very quickly by Private Alston, and not dispatched by Braddis, Leslie promptly took charge.

He went straight to the Norfolks' trench, designated two men as stretcher bearers, and had the body taken to HQ first; he found Dodds's batman trying to fight back tears near the body, and told him gently to go straightaway to his officer's quarters, collect all his possessions in a suitcase—a subaltern would not have many—and deliver them all to the adjutant's office. Then he took Braddis aside; this was not the time to insinuate anything, but to restore some sense of routine order. "You're in

charge of the platoon for the next few days, Sergeant, until we
see what sort of reshufflings we need to do. The men have had a
terrible shock: Lieutenant Dodds was well liked. What they all
need now is a little quiet, to let things settle down, and show
them that things do keep going on, as they have to, and it's not
the end of the world, though they may think it is. But they're not
to be harried by any of us. We'll try to send them something a
little better with their rations. So just keep the regular watches,
but they won't be doing patrols or fatigues or drills for the next
twenty-four hours. Keep yourself ready to talk to the major; he
may be sending for you before the afternoon's out, or later this
evening to get you together with the other platoon commanders; so just make sure you're on the alert through this difficult
transition. There'll certainly be church parade for the company
for a service to honor Lieutenant Dodds and all the others lost
today across the board, so I'll tell the chaplain to be in touch
with you, if he needs details about any of the men lost. One of
our worst days. . . ."

The adjutant went back to his office and arranged to have a
medical officer examine Dodds's body, to find out what was to
be learnt about the nature of his wound, and what sort of
weapon had caused it. It was, Leslie admitted to himself, a kind
of luxury in this war to entertain and examine suspicions about
mere individuals, when what is permanently in your face is the
question of how to thread your fragile way between the imper-
sonal thundering howitzers and forty miles of seven or eight different types of flesh-maiming and -mangling barbed wire. But
Leslie, who had some Yorkshire bloody-mindedness, was not
going to drop his hunch lightly. He could not undo the lawyer in
him; if the world was upside down, and killing had its own
stamped license, it seemed to him a minimal stand for a civilized

authority, if there still was such a thing, to insist that people point their guns the right way. Call it what you like—the case of Dodds would be his own little protest that even in war there is some business worth conducting as normal. He knew he would have to work carefully on this without any help from the company commander, Major Reginald Erskine, who he happened to know from previous comments thought highly of Braddis—the prejudice of one regular soldier for another, for a man who knew the business of war, and did not have to be trained under actual combat conditions how to fight, and perhaps even for a man who shared the same comedy-butt's first name.

Leslie went about his work, but when he returned to his office a half hour later there was already a brief acerbic note from his doctor friend, to the effect that he understood his role was to cure the wounded, so he would not waste much time playing the amateur detective and, besides, he was not equipped for any proper forensic exam. That said, he believed the shot that killed Dodds was fired from a pistol, perhaps a German pistol, with a high-caliber bullet (the sort of death rarely seen at the aid post, and only in the event of close fighting, when men were storming a trench or resisting others storming theirs). He was not going to do a full autopsy, but his probing had brought no trace of fragments of the cartridge, and the size of the exit wound, and the bits of bone around the edge of it, seemed to indicate that the powerful shot fired from close quarters had blasted right through the body. The entry wound, however, was rather neat, a contained puncture of his battle-dress jacket, shirt, and back, and it was his calculation of its slightly larger caliber that indicated a pistol rather than a rifle had fired the shot.

Leslie pondered this one piece of off-the-cuff evidence, trying to resist the next practical step it was urging him to take. The trouble with being placed in a context of maximum uncertainty like war is that the scale of each of your thoughts has now no comparative norm to be measured against, to keep it within bounds, so that there is a risk that any idea can fill your whole empty and nervous head. Leslie, as a careful lawyer, knew this well, but right now the idea was growing within him that he should go and visit the site where Dodds was struck down. By Braddis's own account, the shot was fired not more than fifty yards from the Norfolks' line. He should take that solid Private Alston, who brought the news of his death, and perhaps one other person, so they could show him the route they had withdrawn along—surely they would find some sign of Dodds's fall? Against this in his mind flashed repeatedly a terse warning: you do not go into no-man's-land to play amateur sleuthing. So at this point, the careful adjutant did not know what he would do. He would wait and see if further information or opportunity was forthcoming, to tilt the balance towards action.

Back in his trench, Private Timothy Callum had no doubts about what he thought. And he had no doubts about what he had seen from the moment that Braddis had appeared, stooped but making good time, under the burden of Dodds's body. He had seen a murderer and his victim, a hunter and his trophy over his shoulder; whatever words you laid on the framed picture, Braddis was tied to Dodds, till Judgment Day and past, as slayer to slain. Callum had joined the involuntary rush to the corner of the trench, raised his arms and helped lay the body on the firestep, and he had not felt or allowed himself such a surge of grief as standing over that pale face, since, coming down from the bedroom in the fisherman's cottage when he was ten, where he had been told to stay and read to his brother and sisters till he was called, he had finally been allowed to see his dead mother laid out in the parlor, waiting for her funeral.

But grief was not the only emotion surging through the young soldier; rage had joined it in an equally powerful stream, the one abetting the other. He went and sat next to Charles Alston to unburden himself; the gamekeeper's wise counsel had appeased him when he was losing his grip after a number of lesser affronts from the sergeant. But he did not want appeasing now.

"He killed him, Charlie," he said, managing to keep his voice low. Braddis, who had gone to change his bloodied uniform, had returned to the other end of the trench looking impressively neat and soldierly; he was their platoon commander now, and his bearing would be different. Tomorrow would be Tuesday, but no one would be offering odds on his cutting his nails and sharpening his bayonet in the regular ritual tomorrow.

"We don't know that, Tim."

"I know it, and you know it, and even many of his flunkies know it. The question is, what is anyone going to do about it?"

"Now listen carefully, Tim, because I'm going to say it but once," said Alston with unusual sternness. "A man comes back with a fallen comrade's body is not automatically assumed to have killed him. There were Germans about yesterday, and we lost good men because of them, and we sent them back with bearers. And then comes a last one dead, and he's brought in by a good soldier-sergeant, who saved a lot of our bacon on that day, and we, who were sitting safe back in our trench and never saw a thing, are immediately declaring him the killer. Now, I ask you, is that fair, Tim?"

"It's fair if you know he killed him, and I do. Braddis hated Dodds, because he knew he was on to him, and that he wasn't afraid of him."

"That still doesn't mean he killed him. That's small evidence, Tim."

"So nobody's going to do anything," said Callum, in a detached, bitter voice.

"That doesn't follow either. When Braddis brought the lieutenant in, I thought company HQ should know right away, because there was the question, not just of an officer lost, but of who would command the platoon right now, so I went and told Captain Leslie, the adjutant, and when he heard that it was Braddis brought the body in, his expression turned a little grimlike, and he just said, 'Did he, now?' So I says, 'Yes, sir,' and he says, 'On his own?' and I say again, 'Yes, sir,' and he just turns away, clearly not happy. And I say, if anything follows on now about Braddis and Mr. Dodds, that's the proper place for it to begin, and Captain Leslie is a lawyer, and it will be done proper."

"Well, I'm glad you're satisfied about that, Charlie. But see here now. Everyone says, I just sit here and draw my silly pictures, and take no interest in this great war we are all fighting here, but I'm telling you this right now, Charlie, so you'll know: I'm taking a real interest in this war now, Charlie, and I'm going to look close and make sure things are done right."

"Now, now, Tim. You're young yet, and you're a great artist, Mr. Dodds said, and your main business is to get out of this war alive and well, because you may be able to make things which show a whole lot of people how to look at the world very different from what they see now. So don't you go getting into trouble in the meantime."

"You're a kind man, Charlie, and I know you mean me only good. But the way I see it, Charlie, is we're all in trouble right now."

Callum, having delivered this parting shot, shook his head, and went down the trench and sadly lost himself in a sketch of Braddis delivering the body to the helpers in the trench, a Deposition, he thought, like the ones he'd seen of the poor suffering mother about to receive her crucified son, though you saw nothing of the helpers, except a small forest of weak, dirty, and damaged hands; the whole concentration was on the figure of Dodds, his tunic torn away and a great hole in his pallid, hairless chest and his pale head twisted contortedly askew on his neck, as though in revulsion away from something loathsome; and standing brooding over the delivered body loomed the figure of Braddis, dark, massive but foreshortened, with his bloody hands hooked and clawed in front of him, the telltale finger- and thumbnails dripping blood. Callum was just putting the title over the top of this drawing, "Scavenger Vulture and Victim," when a runner came to Braddis from company HQ, instructing him that Major Erskine was calling a meeting of platoon commanders at 1600 hours, one hour before the battalion meeting— that is, in twenty-five minutes. Callum looked up when he heard Braddis's voice saying he would be there; and then he saw him take out his watch to verify the time. But Callum, noting every word, intonation, and gesture carefully, realized with a shock that the watch Braddis was holding in his hand was the gold watch that Dodds had shown him after telling the story about winning it from his grandfather. Now his assurance about Braddis was made doubly sure in his mind. He tried to curb his fever of certainty, telling himself in Charlie Alston's voice, "A man can be the looter and not the killer"; but the certainty was not a static one, but a stampeding one, and the cautionary thought could not gain ground on it, let alone catch it.

Ten minutes later Braddis went off to his meeting in his new status, and Callum told Alston about Dodds's watch. Alston tried to hold off his own growing, horrified conviction about the sergeant by questioning the boy. Dodds had never shown any gold watch around the trench: where had Callum seen it? And had he just had a quick glimpse, and it might not be the same one? And impatiently Callum told him about the interview he had had with Dodds, who had encouraged him about his art after Braddis had taken two of his pictures, and said there was a kind of get-together of painters and such from the Artists' Rifles every Wednesday at a bar in Armentières, and he would be welcome there, and he could show his drawings to people who knew about art; "and he had this old watch out, that he said he won from his grandfather Augustus Dodds, and I admired it, and he let me hold it, and feel its weight—real hefty it is—in its gold case all sealed up, and its gold chain, and he told me how I could see its face if I pressed the button which held the little winder wheel. So I did that, and you can see I didn't get any quick glimpse, but I got to know the watch and I have a good eye for things. And today I saw Braddis with the same watch and chain, and I saw him press the button on the top, to open the face and read the time, after the runner came from HQ. It's the same watch." And Alston knew it was.

Then, MacIver wrote, there came a swift development arising out of a quirk. (A dying man, he thought, would be held to the strictest laws of probability only up to a point, and God knows, where do quirks occur more frequently than in war?) Giving way to his impulse of indignant curiosity, the methodical Captain Leslie decided to use the absence of Sergeant Braddis from the trench to investigate the supposed crime scene. He would need Private Alston to direct him to the place, and another man would be useful for another pair of eyes and to provide cover. The scene would either reveal something quickly or not at all: fifteen minutes there and back; he was not going to go into the small print of grass stains and soil samples or fibers of cloth. A spent bullet would be useful, a German weapon discarded even better. They would see what was to be seen, and come away. They would enter no-man's-land from the trench of the next section, whose platoon commander was a subaltern Leslie knew and trusted, rather than from Dodds's, where the unsupervised curiosity and gossip about what they were doing would flow freely. The announced mission was to explore the amount of wire damage done by the morning's work, for details to guide future wire parties.

When Leslie summoned Alston and Alston told him about Callum and Dodds's watch, Leslie's hunting instincts started sniffing the air less ambivalently, and he told Alston to get Callum and where they would go. Alston duly went off and returned with Callum, and Leslie briefly checked his story on the details of the watch, his eyes on the boy's face—small, wiry, self-contained, and sharp-eyed, he judged. At the end of his story the young private could not help blurting, "He's sitting there right now, sir, in his meeting with Mr. Dodds's watch in his pocket." Leslie nodded, and said, "Yes. So let's go to work. I'm trusting you, Alston, to lead us to the likely place of Mr. Dodds's death, or at least the close vicinity of it along the path."

"Yes, sir. We've been in and out along that path plenty since we've been up in the line, and I have a shrewd idea where he went down. I'll lead the way, sir, and Private Callum will bring up the rear, and we'll all be moving low, sir, you'll be remember-ing, so we don't start up any firing party."

It was about 1620 when they headed out, with Leslie trying to repress that queasy guiltiness of the prefect at a public school sneaking off for a smoke behind the squash courts with junior boys. The site took no finding at all. Within five minutes, in a small bowl of crater mounds, protected from view from front and behind, the well-trodden path was still stained and wet with blood. That much alone held a horror for all three of them. But all three were good at looking and they started pointing out de-tails to each other. There was a clear sign in the wet imprints of two different shoe sizes, Dodds's from before he crumpled, and the larger ones of Braddis, two prints quite well set in the mid-dle of the path, which might be the point where he took up the burden of Dodds's body. There was a small trail of other human matter strewn forward in the direction from which they had come, but they could not find any trace of the cartridge.

"Never mind that," said Leslie. "I was hoping to find a dis-carded weapon, very possibly a German pistol." He wasn't about to elaborate.

It was Callum who checked the small crater four paces far-ther up the track, off to the right, and found the imprint of Braddis's heels, dry, behind the buttress, and then a full foot-print, wet, facing the little pool of water at the bottom of it. With rising excitement, he called the others over.

"Over here, sir, at this Johnson hole."

"Yes," said Leslie quietly, after a short survey. "The before and the after. This is where he crouched, waiting for Dodds to go by, and this is where he came back and stood, we hope, to throw away his pistol after he killed him, the bottom of his boot bloody. I'm going to ask you, Callum, to step into that pool, very slowly and carefully, and feel around with your boot for any dislodgeable object, pistol sized or larger. It should move if you nudge it. But go very carefully, first because you never know how deep these damn things are, and secondly, because we don't want to stomp the evidence further into the mud."

Callum needed no urging. The pool at the bottom of the crater, for all its steep sides, was only about five feet in diameter, and, it turned out, never more than eight or nine inches deep. The other two watched him in silence, leaving him to explore according to his own system. The water was reflecting a small section of sky before he stepped into it and ruffled the surface. His plan was that he would move first straight across the pool to determine its depth, and then explore the two semicircles to left and right of center. He found the pistol on his first passage, slightly past the center, having nudged it forward in his underwater, ground-level shuffle, and felt it move on.

"There's something right here, sir, about pistol sized," he said tensely.

"Push your sleeve all the way up, and try to pick it up with minimum contact—just a firm grip of thumb and forefinger, if you can."

It was a pistol, and it was, in all likelihood, *the* pistol, as it emerged, completely untarnished, a German 9 mm P08 Luger held in the way Leslie had prescribed, by the bottom of the handle. It had been underwater for less than two hours.

"Excellently done, young Callum," said Leslie. "We will wrap it right here, in this oiled cloth, and take it back for the MPs to tell us what sure information it gives."

He wrapped it gently, and slid it into the pocket of his battle dress.

They were all back in their regular places before 1645. "I must enjoin you both," Leslie said sternly before they parted, "to say nothing about our expedition to anyone at all. You understand?" They did.

Captain Leslie was surprised, on taking his seat, to find that the small group was discussing a wire party that night to repair damage caused during the morning activities; the Germans had made some incursions, and to do that they must have cut some wire. Sergeant Braddis was impressing with his detailed knowledge of the area. "I quite agree, sir," he was saying, "this should not be a big operation at all. I was in on the parties laying most of that wire, and the Germans would certainly not have climbed to any high ground to cut, where they would have been exposed in broad daylight. That leaves the more sunken tracks, and we can check those, repair where needed and get home in short time and good order." The perfect combination of willing and cautious. Major Erskine was entirely happy, though Leslie noticed the other platoon commanders were not liking it, or this Braddis thrust among them.

"Right, then," said the major. "Let's do it. Wire parties to leave at 2200 hours; all safely home by midnight. Nothing daredevil: we've lost too many men today already."

The meeting broke up, and Erskine patted Braddis on the shoulder on his way out, and said, "Welcome to the group, Sergeant. A very useful contribution."

For a long time after this, Leslie searched his soul about his conduct at this meeting and after it, and could not say he had performed well. It is hard to catch the mood of a meeting when you come in very late and have no idea of the developments before; and now it was clear they were accelerating to a close. If he had acted promptly then and there ("Sergeant Braddis, could I see the watch in your pocket?"), as Private Callum would certainly have done, and expected him to do, it would have created quite a stir: there were several people in the room who would recognize it as Dodds's watch, including all his fellow officers probably, and even Erskine. But Braddis was not a fool. He had only to say, "Certainly, sir. Mr. Dodds seemed anxious for me to take it and get it to his family as he was dying, so I was bringing it here to give it to the major, who would know how to handle the matter. It's a lovely old thing." And he would lay it quietly on the table. No sympathy would be lost, certainly from the major, and he, Leslie, would have played a card and had it trumped, before he was ready to present the whole hand. He could, of course, have waited till Braddis was at the door, and therefore leaving with the watch, before making his challenge, but Erskine was the first to leave the room, on his way to the battalion meeting at 1700. The real problem was he had not prepared Erskine for any trouble regarding Braddis, and he was a man who often needed a lot of careful preparation to do the right thing. He was very unlikely to react well to having his meeting transformed into an impromptu courthouse, and his favorite NCO, whom he had just complimented, virtually brought up on charges under his nose. He would regard such a ploy as underhand and subversive, and Leslie could see why. So he was waiting until he could combine Dodds's memo to him, the watch, the sketchy note from the medical officer, and the Luger into one package of evidence. It had been impressed on all of the officers in one of their regular meetings that fingerprints could now establish an individual's identity *with absolute certainty:* that was the sort of evidence he needed. The only question was whether the local detachment of MPs were equipped and trained to handle such evidence. Did they have to send it on to a lab in the hinterland? Would it get there with its vital evidence intact? How many days for a reply? By temperament, as he knew himself, when he asked "the only question," he was always inclined to let another three or four pop out of the envelope.

No, the real problem with Leslie was that, though a competent man and one capable of a bold initiative, as we saw, the basic thrust of his metabolism had been slowed to the cautions and circumambulations of the law's delays; he wanted justice for Dodds, and justice against Braddis. But he did not know how to deliver justice at the pace of war. He left, and made arrangements for the senior military police officer to meet with him tomorrow.

Dodds's platoon, full of baleful speculation and grieving, was driven to fury by the announcement that they would have to return to the ground from which they had been virtually expelled that morning, if only to reinforce wire. It was a broken promise. The adjutant had come and told Braddis that he would be in command, but that the men were not to be troubled with anything besides basic watch duty—no patrols or drills. Now back comes Braddis and says, "Nothing I could do about it, lads. I'm the junior man there. All the officers very keen to repair the damage, and the major went along. Makes sense, of course. When a man knocks a hole in your fence, you don't let it sit unfilled, or you're just inviting him to walk right in when he comes by again. You're not minding your property; you just don't care. Anyway, it's to be out at 2200 and back before midnight, so it's a very limited mission. And the word is there's a rum ration thrown in with tea."

They were so easily bought off. Men with small expectations, smaller sense of entitlement. But not Callum. His rage was now boundless, and it was not on any union grounds of a clause in the contract reneged on. His outrage proceeded from the single fact that Braddis was still in command, which could only mean that Captain Leslie had done precisely nothing. Which was in fact true. And for Callum that led coldly and directly to only one conclusion. Alston saw the thunder in his face, and came to try and calm him down. "Don't say one thing, Charlie," said Callum. "I gave him the fucking pistol that shot Dodds. I just don't get it. He goes into a room and sits down at the table, with the pistol that shot Dodds in his pocket; across the table sits Braddis, who had used the pistol, and is sitting with the watch in his pocket, which he had got by using the pistol. So in one room, you have the killer and thief, the weapon he used to kill, and the ill-gotten gains of his killing, and another man who outranks him and knows all these things and does bugger all—except maybe talk about wire. So what's he going to do with the gun, anyway?"

"He's giving it to the military police, to get the fingerprints off it—which should nail him down good."

"How long'll that take?"

"I don't know about these things. Maybe a couple of days."

"A couple of days we don't have. You know enough to know that Braddis should be under arrest as we speak, instead of being promoted to command the platoon; and a full investigation under way to find what's left of the bullet, which was fired from that gun we gave them, and will have some of Dodds's blood on it. Don't go all dumb on me, Charlie. You know that ought to be happening, before the evidence gets removed or destroyed by rain, or trampled into the mud by a fucking wire party."

"Yes, you're right, Tim. It should."

But the conversation had cleared Callum's mind, and a little venting of his frustration had cheered him up considerably; he was now looking forward to the evening's wire party. In fact, Callum and his adversary Braddis were probably the most enthusiastic about the coming escapade; Callum was sorting out his own purposes, and Braddis was looking for another chance to do what he did best, and this time in command, so the spotlight would be on him. He was where he wanted to be, and he would look after his men and show real savvy, and bring them all home safe. He was feeling positively benign, basking in his major's approval.

So at 2200 the Norfolks took to the field again, this time encumbered with picks, shovels, coils of revetting wire, fierce-pronged staples, pine stakes, and picket mauls to drive them home. The sergeant would lead the wire party, because he was the only one who knew what did or did not need doing, and Private Alston would lead the cover group, though they would help with the carrying, going out. After the morning, they were down to two sections now. Braddis addressed them all in the trench before they went:

"All right, lads, piece of cake. We're going to go slow, low and methodical. No talking, except to your mate on the exact job in hand, and very short, quiet talk even then. Remember, if the stakes are sound, you don't have to drive in new ones. You just have to wrap new wire across the gaps and staple it home. Too much hammering and you-know-who wakes up."

They went out on a starry night under a quarter moon. It was as smooth as Braddis, the lucky old professional, had said it would be. Only four strands were cut, and Braddis knew where they were likely to be, so there was no aimless roaming up and down the wire to find the gaps. By 2310 the work was done, and they regrouped around the sergeant. "Right, lads," he said softly. "We've locked the gate and swept the porch, and we're going back inside."

Private Alston led them back, the wire party following, still encumbered with its tools and most of its materials, then the cover group, and then Sergeant Braddis, the platoon commander. He had in mind, before they set out, to stop off at the point of his fateful encounter with Dodds that afternoon on his return, just to confirm that everything was shipshape, but he was now feeling that was unnecessary: forty-two individual boots had stomped up that narrow path on the way out, and the same forty-two on the way back; if it was a crime scene, it was already a very well trampled one. Besides, he was conscious that any delay in his return would start prompting thoughts of his late return earlier; the men were feeling good about his sure touch on this patrol—he should join them promptly, thank them for their good work, wish them a sound good-night, and let them look forward to more good times under his kindly management tomorrow. Right now, Braddis was feeling in a more euphoric state than he had at any time perhaps since he had hoisted the King's hefty silver trophy for the services champion marksman at Bisley.

Private Callum was also in an altered and surprisingly euphoric state during the patrol: he had worked out exactly what he was going to do, and he was certainly not going to do it in the cowardly way that Braddis had disposed of Dodds. When the moment came, it seemed there was a great, spreading ease of opportunity given him by good luck alone: it would be simpler for him now, because Charlie Alston had been sent on ahead to lead the withdrawal and would not be around to keep an eye on him, when he followed with the rest of his section behind the wire party.

Callum had chosen another rampart conveniently molded by the earth-moving sculpture of an exploding artillery shell, about twenty yards farther on from the Norfolks' lines than the smaller Johnson hole where Braddis had waited. Callum had thought that Braddis might well linger around the earlier site, and lingering men are more on their guard. He was third to last of the cover section to leave the wire, and when he got level with his rampart he stopped to retie the dragging bootlace he had untied before he left. The other two, impatient to be back, were about to swear at his delay, but he told them to go on ahead. "It doesn't matter what fucking order we arrive in, for Chrissake." He had not more than ten seconds to hide himself, take the bayonet from its scabbard, fix it to his rifle, and take his position. He did it in seven, no record time but quite creditable.

Braddis came down the path at his regular, light-footed speed, even whistling to himself under his breath. Callum had calculated from watching him move in battle that he would be almost upright in this enclosed space, and he was. Callum was into him as he was drawing level, with a deep thrust into the belly and then upwards under the thorax to pierce the heart. It was a move Braddis had taught them all at bayonet practice in the Bull Ring at Rouen, before they went up to the line, but the sergeant was not quite ready for it now. He dropped the maul he was carrying in his left hand, and grabbed Callum's rifle ahead of the bayonet, pulling himself onwards to reach the attacker. Callum, with clenched teeth, was watching the big, heavy man coming at him, holding on for dear life, and in some dread that those awful nails might get close enough to close on his jugular. Braddis was looking at him with half-closed eyes, and said in an almost normal voice: "So, finished me, have you, young Callum, with an up-and-under from below, easy as tossin' hay in summer? . . . Your friend Dodds's watch is in my left pocket here, and he might want you to have it. . . ." Callum allowed his eyes to flicker for a half second towards Braddis's tunic, and in the same moment Braddis had his bayonet in his right hand, and used it to slice deep into Callum's left leg, and drag it upwards, gouging the hipbone, and then sinking the razor-sharp, attenuated blade deep into the lower bowel of the boy's stomach.

With a final, galvanized spasm of his full strength, Callum managed to throw the sergeant backwards with the rifle and bayonet still in him. The bayonet was sticking out of his back, but the fall dislodged it, and the weapon quite slowly collapsed on top of him. Braddis was dead, and Callum knew he had a fatal wound, too, but was still riding the high tide of exultation at what he had done. He moved quite deliberately, holding his stomach. He found the watch where Braddis had told him, and he managed to remove the bayonet from his rifle, and left it lying there. Then, using the rifle as a prop, he headed out deeper into no-man's-land.

CHAPTER 12

The Deserter in No-Man's-Land

Tim Callum could not go far in his condition, but he made it about seventy yards, the last part of it off the track into yet more cratered terrain. This was near where he and Private Alston had been covering for some of the wire party an hour ago, and he had made a point of saying to Charlie he thought it might make a good hideaway; he was hoping Charlie would come looking for him soon. Not that he wanted Charlie to take him in: that was the very last thing he wanted. But he expected he would be dead by morning, and he wanted to talk to him before he died.

He lay down carefully on the gradual slope of his chosen crater; it certainly hurt to bend, and he didn't intend to move again. He had his rifle and his water bottle next to him, and that was all he would need now. He could feel his stomach distending as it was filling up with something that he hoped was blood. In the grisly talk of the trenches, on the theme of terrible ways to go, someone had mentioned people having their intestines pierced and their stomach cavity filling up with their own shit, and poisoning their blood, so that days later they died of something like gangrene. He had no intention of lingering to die of anything so obscene. But above all he would not let Charlie take him back.

Meanwhile, less than ten minutes had gone by, but most of the men and certainly Private Alston were already aware that neither Sergeant Braddis nor Private Callum had returned. He sent a runner to the orderly room to tell Captain Leslie that both of them were missing in action, and that he personally was going back with two other men to try to find them. So for the third time within eighteen hours, the three of them were stalking the access lanes of no-man's-land.

They found Braddis where he lay, his custom-tailored bayonet still in his right hand, and presumably Callum's blood on it, and Callum's regular one alongside it. Blood and white nooses of intestine had bubbled out of the extended gash in Braddis's tunic. For several moments, they were all silent in shock. Then Private Rhys, for the sake of filling the void, said, "If you were a betting man, you'd have to have said it would go the other way." And his friend Jim Berry said, "Yes. He must have taken him sudden, maybe coming out from there; but he took him from the front, man to man, not with a bullet in the back."

"Amen to that," said Alston. "Now you two need to go back and choose two good friends for a stretcher party, take Braddis back and try to keep the place from going hog wild with talk and rumor. Some hope. If Captain Leslie is there, tell him I've gone to look for Callum, but I will be back within thirty minutes." He was taking charge.

They went back for their friends and the stretcher, and Alston went on to find Callum. He knew where he was. He found him on the slope of the crater, still leaking a lot of blood from his leg and stomach. A small stream of it was flowing down between his legs, had reached the bottom of the slope, and was mixing with the large puddle on the crater floor. He was pale as a ghost, but lying still and not yet in much pain, and he wanted to talk.

"I knew you would come. Some first things first, Charlie. I've got right here Mr. Dodds's watch, and I want you to take it and make sure it goes back to his grandfather, who gave it to him, Augustus Dodds, who lives somewhere on the Bure River in Norfolk. It's all right if you give it to Captain Leslie to pass on, because he may be able to get it there quicker, but you'll impress on him that it's to go to no one else. Now the second thing is, when you get back to Norfolk yourself, I want you to visit my dad and the children, you'll like them, and just talk to them simple as you can and tell them I died honorable. But I want you to visit Ann Houghton, my old teacher from the local school, in person, and give her my sketchbook, which you'll find in the top left-hand pocket of my battle-dress tunic. Don't bother my dad with it, because he never cared much about art and stuff, never had the time for it. But I'd like Miss Houghton to know I did good for her. Will you do these things for me?"

"You know I will. To the letter."

"Yes, you will. You know, Charlie, I don't regret one bit what I did tonight. I'm proud of it, and I'll tell you why. Mr. Dodds recognized me, and encouraged me, through all this shit of the war, and I wasn't going to let him die unavenged. And I wasn't going to wait till I could do nothing about it. Do you blame me?"

"No, I don't think I do. You're not me. You're an avenging angel, and there's a lot of anger fuels you. If you had been my son, you'd probably come with more caution; but you wouldn't have been able to do half the things you do."

"Not an avenging angel, Charlie. I like to think I'm a very little bit like Odysseus, the Greek, whose name means something about sorrow. I was crazy about him when I read him in school. And when he was a boy he went to visit his granddad, who lived on Mount Parnassus where Apollo and the Muses live; they was doing nothing but art, as I understand it, and everything was beautiful. But unfortunately there was this huge rampaging wild boar messing things up and eating people; and Odysseus went out and hunted him. And the boar just erupted out of the thicket, but Odysseus was ready, and got his spear into him, with an underthrust, and held on for dear life, but the weight of the boar was on him, and he got his tusk into the boy's leg before he died, and Odysseus carried the scar for the rest of his life, as I will Braddis's. I was going to do a picture of it. The spear in the boar, and the tusk in the boy, all balanced. But too late. End of story."

"I never heard that story before."

"It's there, right in the book. . . . I'm a little afraid of dying out here, Charlie, but you're not under any circumstances going to let them take me back in, and patch me up, and have me shot for killing their fucking sergeant. I am going to die here, Charlie."

"Yes, I know."

"You remember all those spooky stories about where deserters went? They can't go back behind their lines, because they'll be shot, and they can't go over to the other side, because they despise them and will probably shoot them too, so they all head out into no-man's-land, and live wild lives, banding together in packs like wolves and scavenging for food and stuff off the dead and wounded bodies. Do you believe that?"

"No, I don't. And you took on Braddis—he was more than a pack of deserters."

"That's true. And I've got my rifle right here in case. It's time you headed back, or else they'll think I killed you too, and come looking for you. Take the things."

So Charles Alston took the watch and sketchbook and put them in his pockets, and left him his own water bottle and some chocolate.

"Will you come and see me again?"

"Yes, I will. About two in the morning. That's a bit more than two hours from now."

He went back and found Captain Leslie fretting and waiting for him.

"This has been the most disastrous day," the Captain said.

"Disastrous and long, sir," said Alston.

"Yes, I'm sorry, you look all in. Tell me what you know."

"Better to talk in private, sir."

They went to Leslie's office, where under the light, noticing Alston's haggard state, he poured him a whisky, and took one himself. Leslie sat behind the desk, and Alston in a chair beside it. They were going to talk it out. Throughout, Leslie was conscious that the disparity in their rank, between captain and private, meant nothing, outweighed by a kind of moral force in Alston, which he did not feel in himself.

Leslie wanted to know where Callum was, and made it clear that he wanted him brought in to face charges: "This is not an army where you kill your sergeant with impunity."

Alston would not tell him where Callum was. "And besides, sir, it's irrelevant. He was badly wounded, and is quite likely dead while we speak. He will never live to face charges."

"Do you know why he killed Braddis?"

"Yes, sir, I do, though it will make hard hearing for you. He was afraid it might be an army where a sergeant could kill his platoon commander with impunity. He knew you were in the room with Braddis, and that you had the gun he had used to kill Dodds in your pocket, while Braddis had Dodds's watch in his. And you told us Mr. Dodds had warned you about Braddis. And young Tim could not understand how with this evidence, nothing was done; in fact, back comes Braddis on top of the world, promoted to platoon commander. As Callum said, you had the killer, the weapon, the loot in the room with you, and you did nothing. There should at least have been a full investigation launched, and Braddis held under suspicion while it was being conducted, Callum thought. As it was, we were going to send the whole platoon back stomping on the evidence out there." Leslie was looking uncomfortable, and was about to protest. But Alston held up his hand to stop him. "No, sir, you don't have to account for your actions; I know there is a regular process for these situations, which you would understand and I don't, and I know you would have to consult Major Erskine and all that. I'm just explaining to you what Tim was thinking: he was an angry boy, and he could not wait—he decided he had to deal with Braddis himself."

"Which he did savagely and bravely. I wouldn't take Braddis on with a bayonet."

"Nor I, sir. He was a brave lad all right, but I think it was a matter of pride for him, that he take him on from the front, and not shoot him from behind."

"But I don't quite see why the degree of his passion. Why, to put it baldly, was he so for Dodds and so against Braddis?"

"It was personal on both fronts, sir. Braddis used to persecute

Callum—Tim was a very skilled artist, and would keep to himself and draw things, and for some reason Braddis hated that, and would take his drawings, and we once saw him tear one up in front of all of us; whereas Mr. Dodds recognized Tim's talent and encouraged him, and he was always grateful to him for it. I think Mr. Dodds may also have rebuked Braddis about it."

Leslie saw that the tired man had thought through this mess far straighter than he could, and that the conclusions he arrived at would be the right ones; instinctively, he began to feel that if he was to emerge with any self-esteem from the matter himself, he should take his own stand with Alston and should campaign with him honorably, against Erskine and any others, in Alston's straightforward manner. "Where do we go from here?" he said.

"Well, sir," said Alston, "I have the luxury of being able to say what I think, without being held responsible for it. So there are three points I would like to mention. The first is that I think you know if there was ever an inquiry, and I was called to it, I would not lie under oath on any point. I am hoping very much there will be no inquiry, because I think we would all emerge looking bad and learning nothing from it. If I was the major, which we're all happy I'm not, the official status of the three deaths would be 'killed in action' for both Dodds and Braddis, and 'missing in action, presumed dead' for Callum. As I see it, this is a case where we leave the Almighty to assign the blame.

"The second point comes out of this. It's important that Callum have an honorable 'missing in action, presumed dead' title, so the pension will be paid to his father, who is a very poor fisherman with three young children to support. That would be bringing some good out of the evil. We all know Mr. Dodds is entirely innocent and a very good officer, and he should have every honor. But I would leave Braddis and Callum equally unblemished, as it were, in their eye-for-an-eye furies—at least on the official record."

"And the third point?"

"Yes. The third point concerns Mr. Dodds's watch. You remember, we were all confident that the watch was in Sergeant Braddis's pocket, and it was there when he was killed. I have it here." And he put it on Leslie's desk. "Tim Callum, ever since he saw Braddis look at it in the trench, was very strong for the notion that the watch should go back to Mr. Dodds's grandfather, Augustus Dodds, who gave it to him. I think he lives in Norfolk, if he's still alive, somewhere on the Bure River. Tim thought that you, sir, would be the best one to handle that. It's clearly a valuable old thing, and he was sure you would be the one to see that it got to old Mr. Dodds and no one else."

Captain Leslie felt surprised and oddly proud to have been considered an honorable man for such a mission. "I certainly will see to it," he said formally. And in a more relaxed style added, "You've been enormously helpful to me, Alston. You should go and get some sleep."

"Thank you, sir."

At the door, the adjutant could not help asking one more question: "Do you ever wonder how we all get into these horrible predicaments?"

"Ah, that's the big one, sir, isn't it?" said Private Alston. "There'll be no sleep for either of us, if we talk that one out. But I would hazard it has to do something with the war, of course, and behind that, the angers that give wars their status, and stoke us all up to behave awry. Otherwise, I can't help you."

So Charles Alston went out, not to bed, but to visit young Tim Callum, as he had promised. He took a trenching tool, and told the sentry on watch to keep alert and not to shoot him going or coming. As he had expected, the boy had died while he was away. His rifle was still beside him, and he had not had to use it. Alston dug a grave for his friend, as deep as he could, and laid him in it with his rifle and water bottle, covered it up, smoothed the soil, and said a short prayer over it. As always, a quiet, methodical man. Then he went home to sleep.

CHAPTER 13

His Own Quietus

MacIver did not now know how many days had gone into the writing of the last day of Dodds, Braddis, and Callum, how many suppers left uncooked, or cooked and left uneaten, how many fires laid, lit, and left to die untended. Tiny images swam in and out of his ken, like the magnolia buds in their cocoons of ice tap-tapping on the window beside his bed as he lay there. In full dress in the spring, the motion would be a sustained swaying of their waxy torches brushing the glass soundlessly. But now everything edgy, as it were nervously short-measured. He had a faint memory, as from the distant past, of being on the floor trying to cut up the board of a bookshelf to make kindling. For some reason he was using his folding Opinel country knife, rather than the more serviceable hatchet—he must have mislaid it. The knife was not equal to the job, but in his forcing of it, he nicked the skin between thumb and forefinger quite deep; it was not painful, but blood was demonstratively cascading onto the wood and the floor. Suddenly he was wracked with sobs, and starting stabbing the board in a frenzy, on and on, as the blood and chips of wood flew everywhere. But afterwards when he looked down at the wound, he saw it as a clean little hole in the loose skin, a small fish-mouth of a wound, which opened and shut when he moved his thumb. Who would have thought the old man had so much blood in him? It happened quite spontaneously, and was certainly embarrassing to him as he thought about it afterwards; he decided the outburst, or tantrum rather, was both his last display of grief for Margaret gone, and David gone, and the loss of all good people, things, and times; and it was also his last spasm of self-pity at the actual moment of his own life giving way to impotence. It would not be long now.

He did not intend to write another line, but he could still take an interest in the characters he had created; there was some pleasure in projecting their lives further out, or going forwards and backwards over them, as memory does with our own, or pondering their contradictions. So in the evening of the day on which he finished his story, he sat on in the rocking chair with the rug across his knees, and tied up the little fraying threads of his ending. The public television station was making a civilized drone at low volume across the room. Now that he was not laying words on the page, to his surprise he found he rather liked the human voice in its quietest mode.

But his thoughts were all back in the trenches, in April 1917. What might happen next? Simon Dodds's platoon was so decimated and seemingly cursed by now that MacIver saw it being withdrawn to reserves, and the men redistributed after leaves to other companies. Captain Leslie played a large part in getting Private Alston both decorated and swiftly advanced to sergeant. Both of them had the temperament and marks of men who would survive the war: they would have their *nostos*.

MacIver watched Leslie return Simon Dodds's watch to his grandfather Augustus on his next leave. He imagined that the exchange would be over tea on the porch, because that was the setting for the gift to Simon in the first place, and Augustus would have a strong sense of occasion. Leslie would be pleased to see the old man spring the case open, check the time, close it, and slip it into the little pocket of his waistcoat, in the familiar moves of all old men with a pocket watch. The ancient rhythms restored with simplicity. Then they sat on, and Leslie told Augustus about his friend Simon as an officer, sparing him the harshness of his end; and afterwards the gravity gave way to more relaxed conversation and good talk about sailing. Leslie might even stay to supper, and spend the night in the guest room, with the river finding its way below the window; and then take the morning train back to Whitby.

MacIver, rocking quietly over his Lagavulin, also attended Alston's sweet, sad visit to Callum's family; he had brought presents for all of them, and the children brought him drawings that Tim had done of each of them, and of lively animals pictured on rainy days. And again, in an easier setting, he looked over Ann Houghton's shoulder as she leafed through the sketchbook, and was delighted when Alston, sitting opposite her, insisted that she explain to him what was finely wrought in each of the drawings—what made Tim a real artist. He was older than all her students, she thought, but there weren't many more motivated to learn.

This was pleasant enough, but sentiment for MacIver the Scot was always prone to a critical aftertaste. He wanted to ponder the parables he had made for himself in the character of the adversaries Braddis and Callum. Alston had talked to Leslie of "anger giving war status," but he was a gentle man, and *anger* was too mild a word. *Rage* was the necessary word, perhaps the first word onto the page in Western literature with Achilles' *menis* in the *Iliad.* The warriors sitting in the halls listening to the stories Homer told would understand it—the unconsidered savagery that made soldiers and hunters kill on reflex, implacable, with no hesitant thought of the circumstances, bloodlust without concern for propriety or question of right timing. And the license seems given to rage to stay rampant, even when the killing has stopped. The gods themselves understand that Achilles is entitled to drag the body of Hector around his city's walls in front of his grieving family, for his own honor's sake, his *kleos;* at least, they allow it for three days, and then they call a halt to it. Achilles must show his graciousness before the end—it is only right. Cúchulain must be boiled in the huge vat of a bath to drain the rage out of him and make him fit for society again. But how absurd to imagine that the public causes of war stoke the rage to their highest point, rather than the private grievances. Achilles himself makes it clear he has no part in and no particular feeling about Agamemnon's and Menelaus's little embarrassment; he has nothing against the Trojans. Let his honor be affronted, and let him lose his soulmate Patroclus, and you will find out what anger really is.

MacIver had given rage to both Braddis and Callum. On a first look, Callum might be saved from the worst aspects of it by his art, his "grim and hard pictures," as they would be, as long as he painted for himself. But Braddis was certainly a performance artist of a kind, and a rare one too, with the rituals of his nails and his bayonet, and especially his athletic sureness on the killing fields. MacIver knew these men, and he had given them qualities that were in himself, and he believed they survived dangerously even in societies that count themselves civilized.

A good scholar had once told MacIver that she believed that every great epic has planted within it the seeds of a critique of the ideology that drives the narrative. So in the case of the *Iliad*, poor Hector knows that glory demands that he go out on the battlefield to meet Achilles, *mano a mano*, while his gentle wife Andromache urges him that if he really wants to save his family, why doesn't he simply defend them from the unassailable walls of Troy? And at the end, when Hector is dead and all is lost, she cries in her lament: why could you not have died in bed next to me, holding out your arms and telling me some personal thing, which I would remember all the days of my grieving? Now there, thought MacIver, is a radical counterideology: what is wrong with dying in bed?

It is the real women who gentle our condition, finding their pleasures close to them, as they go about their work, like everyone else, getting through the day. Without them, we are all rampaging in Braddis Land. In his own life, he knew it was Margaret who pulled him back from the blood-and-guts, slash-and-burn pillage party he had been mentally shaping for himself in his dry little corner of academe. She was the Muse who tamed the wild boar on Parnassus, the unicorn in the gardens of Aquitaine.

MacIver wondered if Callum, in the short time he lay waiting for his end in no-man's-land on that soft spring night in Flanders, reached an end of his rage, and saw beyond it. He knew that Callum had taken up Simon Dodds's suggestion that he should one evening join the artists in their noisy bar in Armentières. It had taken courage, of which Callum had plenty, to do it. Paul Nash had been there, still just on the point of hammering himself into an artist who saw things differently. On that level, he and Callum were quite well matched, with Callum the better draughtsman of the two. But Nash was an officer, and capable of being a snotty and neurotic one, and besides, he had connections already in the art world, though not necessarily better than Callum's Miss Houghton. All of this, though, quite intimidating, one would have thought, to a boy, a mere private, out of school since sixteen, who had never set foot in an art school and may not have known there were such things. But not intimidating to Callum; he would not have to make conversation. He shouldered to the bar, got himself a beer, squeezed into the last chair in a noisy, crowded corner, and went to work, doing what came naturally, sketching the faces around him, some with big names already shaped, or to be attached to them in the near future, though he would know nothing of that. Soon they were crowding around him like bees to the honeypot, the gentle David Jones, Private John Ball himself, and indeed Paul Nash, thick jet-black hair brushed straight back clear of the forehead to emphasize the pale blue eyes and the strong aquiline nose; and also his brother, the landscapist John Nash.

They asked to see the sketchbook, and passed it around as he sat watching them, quietly sipping his beer. They admired the sure strength of line, sometimes the effortless ferocity of three or four telling strokes, bringing a man past falling to a tortured collapse. And Paul Nash made a confession that he had always wanted to draw like that, but that he had no confidence that he could do it and keep it spare; he had started with little pastoral pictures of silent gardens, full of weeping trees with fussy, thin lines, and nobody around them. "But when I came to the trenches, I had to tell myself, 'Unthink pretty. Where do you think you are? Rub your eyes, boy. Now look again!' And yet, you know, Tim"—whose name he had just learnt—"when you grow familiar with these trenches, God help me, I find there's a kind of beauty of their own—even what happens to the smoke of artillery at sunset, after the big guns have defoliated another copse or wood. The smoke adds another shape and another color

mass to catch the fading light. So there's nature, and then there's
what we have done to nature, the reverse of it, as it were, and I
find myself doubly enthralled." So Callum had a good evening,
and when he was leaving, they urged him to come again, and he
said he would, and there was a moment, as he was walking away,
when he imagined that peace might come one day, and they
would all be back in England working at their art without patrols or wire parties. But then, almost at once, he realized that he
would not go back. He had things he had to do, and they would
bring it all to an end.

But what about now, my hard, fierce boy? urged MacIver.
How do you feel, as you lie waiting to die from your fatal
wound? Do you see a nobler chance beyond the grim and hard?
What would Callum say right now, lying still so as not to hurt
under his quarter moon?

The question pulled MacIver up short for a bit, but in the
end he imagined that Callum would stay, not hard, but firm: You
want a happy ending, MacIver, you want it all to add up to one
big thing, the good and the bad, the plus and the minus, the nature and the violence to nature. Well, good luck, I suppose, but
I can't do it. Listen to this, MacIver, you big dumb Scot: the
hardest thing anyone can do is to tell other people, or anyone
else, by whatever means, *exactly what he sees*. Not his own version
of what he sees shaded according to little bits of what someone
else sees; just what he sees himself. That's all I've tried to do, and
all I wanted to do. So if you don't like it, as Ben Winterbourne
would say, Fuck off, MacIver.

Certainly, thought MacIver politely, because the boy was
some kind of genius. The most distilled, frightening form of
single-mindedness. And yet. The fact is that we do learn from
each other, especially those we admire or love. That is perhaps

why we have schools. We can come, if we are blessed, to see things differently, because we've been shown a better look. Captain Leslie was going to chase after young Tim Callum and throw the book at him, which is what army regulations and the law specified should be done. But then Private Alston sits next to him, and in a quiet tidy way shows him the whole matter can stop right here, and everyone better for it. And Leslie takes the view as his own, because it's better. And also perhaps because, quite apart from this particular judgment, there was a larger one: the fact is that Leslie knows Alston is a better man than he is, and he wants to be like him.

MacIver was fairly sure that he did not understand how the alchemy of changing a spirit works. The odd thing was that his gentle, spirited Margaret *liked* him angry, as long as he didn't demean or consume people. She liked the way he exploded through the jammed door, as though there were nothing there; there was no conspicuous adjustment of his person, no visible lowering of the shoulder or anything. He just went through the door, and the door, as though it knew what was coming, had to efface itself, and flattened itself against the adjacent wall.

One day, at least ten years ago, he reckoned, Margaret had appeared in his little summer study from across the yard, with a beautifully lettered poster she had made of a line of Blake. "This is not just for you, it is you," she said. The line read:

THE TYGERS OF WRATH ARE WISER THAN THE
HORSES OF INSTRUCTION.

"If I was a simply adoring nineteenth-century wife, I would have made it a sampler for you, sighing over every stitch, but I don't have the time. But I feel just as she does."

"What a wonderful thing!" exclaimed MacIver. "But what exactly *is* the wisdom of the Tyger, do you think?"

"Isn't that the question? I think Blake would say, if you are as beautifully balanced and symmetrical in every way as the Tyger (and only if you have a *y* in your name, remember), then your hair-trigger instincts bring you out ahead of any amount of laborious calculation."

"I'm going to spell MacIver with a *y* from now on, I think. But I once met a tiger, who told me his wisdom consisted in the perception that the world is full of shit and assholes, and the only judgment that stands up is the one that declares 'It's all crap!'—which were incidentally the 'Angelic Doctor' Thomas Aquinas's dying words."

"I doubt if Aquinas said exactly that, but that is exactly the sort of disreputable tiger you would meet. And I notice you spelt him with an *i*."

"I noticed he was very, very popular with the tigresses, however."

MacIver sat on rocking in his chair, drowsing now and then, on another blessed day of absolution from pain, and sipping the last of the warm maple syrup and the Lagavulin in the glass beside him when he remembered. Now the exchange with Margaret over the Blake poster pushed him still further back, before they were together. There had been a brief period in the thirties, when MacIver had been doing research in Paris, and arrangements were made for him to play rugby for the Paris University Club, whose cheer was, and is, *Allez PUC!* (pronounced with a long French *u* and hard *c*), and whose public address system introduced him as L'Ecossais Sensationnel, which, as people were fond of pointing out to him, sounded a whole lot better than "the Sensational Scot." The point of the memory, however, was the character of the physiotherapist who helped him with various muscle tears and other things over this short season. Her name was Claudine, and she came, she said, from Provence, and was a half gypsy (*une demi-tzigane*). This exotic makeup, according to hearsay, accounted for her uncannily knowing hands and touches over the human body, though her sister Ariane had told MacIver that she did not have a drop of gypsy blood in her, but had adopted the persona when she was five to annoy their mother, a very proper lady from Seville. MacIver preferred Claudine's version and filled in details of her history for himself: he imagined that when the colorful, painted caravans pulled over onto the deserted field beside the stream, and the stocky horses, mongrels, and healthy, dirty children were all released to crop grass and play, the young women would gather around the ancient, far-seeing, and vaguely menacing grandmothers, and there learn the secret uses of herbs, lotions, unguents, and incantations, where and when to be applied, to what parts of the body, at which phases of the moon.

Claudine certainly liked playing on the mysterious aspects of her work, and MacIver was crazy about it. He never stepped on a rugby field in better fettle than after he had been tended by her. She was striking to look at, but not conventionally beautiful. Long and lean would be a summary phrase, applying to face, arms, hands, legs, feet, and the whole assemblage of the parts (she cannot have been more than an inch under six feet), but it does not convey one jot of how womanly she was. A torrent of black hair and eyes almost as dark under jet-black eyebrows, surprisingly delicate nose and lips. Smoothly shaded complexion and skin, unhelpfully described as a rosy olive color. She had very little hair on her body.

This last detail was a known fact from the final procedure in any session with her, for which she would undress and lie next to MacIver, who first lay on his stomach with his arms stretched out above him, and then on his back with his arms still raised. Claudine stressed that her nudity was essential for the protocol to work, because it reduced the dangerous "tension of reserve." Her procedure was to touch his body all over, with variations of pressure, from feathery light to stressful sharpness with finger-tips, hands, sometimes lips, but mostly with her long nails, which she would slide under the hair on his belly and chest and down all the slopes and planes of his body. But the most impor-tant and dramatic element of the procedure was the repeated chant of the single injunction "No, don't hurt this flesh" (*Non, ne blessez pas cette chair*), invariably starting low and whispering gentle, but then rising through every variation—urgency, agita-tion (*Non, non, non, non, ne blessez* . . .), low moaning, harsh cries, and sometimes sobs, before touching down again in gen-tleness. Sex was never mentioned by either of them, let alone discussed, but it was often enacted, and sometimes more than once, in the course of this unvarying ritual. MacIver always tried to get Claudine to talk about the chant, but she would look at him in some consternation and say, "But it is quite obvious—it's a song to ward off evil (*une chanson apotropaïque*)!"

Margaret loved Claudine, whom of course she never met, and she loved her procedures, at which she became a talented practitioner. But she loved her most for what she called her "generous playacting, so wholehearted that both of you were caught into the drama, and probably believed it. So don't belit-tle it now. I can assure you that 'Don't hurt this flesh' is a mantra every woman says, at least to herself, from the time she is bathing her baby, to holding her lover, to sending her man off to war."

I have to conclude, MacIver said to himself, that Margaret was the only completely passionate, completely gentle person I ever met. And to think I almost lost her.

That evening, perhaps undeservedly, MacIver, who had had some recognition in his life, was given a final award. He had dozed, tottered off to see if he could squeeze a few more drops out of the empty Lagavulin bottle into his glass, added some warm water, and managed to climb back into his rocker without spilling it. He was now inhaling its peaty vapors, rather than drinking it. All of this took some concentration, and it was only by accident that his attention was suddenly caught by something on television. The sound was on just loud enough for him to catch a particular voice and recognize it. And upon inspection, it turned out that he knew that woman on the screen.

He had the TV tuned to the public channel, and there was a book program on. The interviewer, dapper but determinedly faceless, was skillfully feeding his guest lines without comment or judgment, giving her enough rope to soar or hang herself on her own. The young woman was doing wonderfully well. She was a former student of his, Katherine Corton, a quiet beauty. MacIver did not know her well. She had taken his course on World War I in graduate school, but her own field was American history. She had excelled for him, and he had been happy to be added to her dissertation committee—she had asked for him, because her work, like his, had made use of oral history. The thesis had been on the Depression, called *Together in Hardship;* and its boldest claim, as he remembered it, was that that decade, far more than any periods of prosperity, had reawakened the country to its founding document, the Constitution: Americans at the lowest ebb, living hard, rediscovered after a long sleep, that not only did they have rights, but they were meant to be bound together in solidarity against whatever assailed them all; they should all have a sense of personal entitlement, and had been given strong words to insist that the miserable conditions of their world should change.

The big sweep of this thesis, MacIver remembered, had caused grave consternation among the microspecialists at the time Ms. Corton defended it. But she had disarmed them all by the subtlety of the qualifications she had shaded in, and by the wonderful profusion of instances of collective enterprise and mutual support she had gathered in that period, from the unlikeliest sources. It certainly had not hurt her with her dissertation committee that she was soft-voiced and beautiful: whatever the supposed erudition and objectivity of their research, these were at root, he knew, fairly primitive men, like himself.

Once past the hurdle of the defense, the thesis had immediately won attention and awards: it offered both optimism and a long continuity of positive purpose in the country, and thinking people were glad of both. She was well on her way, and it turned out that the occasion for the present interview was the Bancroft Prize for outstanding work in American history, which she had just received for her latest book. MacIver was glad to see her, a lovely visitor from his former world; she seemed quite unchanged and unspoiled—the same gracious consideration of each question she was answering, the same appreciation of the complexity of things, the same obvious humanity, and with all of it, the same capacity to make firm, telling judgments. She told you things you did not know. A brilliant woman. MacIver felt absurdly proud and happy for her.

At the end, it turned out they had a surprise for him. It was hard to tell with an interviewer so systematically inscrutable, but MacIver thought he betrayed his delight in his guest by concluding with a fat question she could play with: which scholars would she consider she was most influenced by, in her scholarly methods and her writing? She could make or dash reputations with her answer.

A pause to consider, and then, of course, another generous reply. She had been very fortunate in her teachers; and she named them. "But," she continued, "I would have to say that far and away the most important lesson I learned for my profession was taught to me by Robert MacIver."

The interviewer had to dig far down in his memory, but, clearly surprised, came up with the right man: "The historian of the First World War?"

"Yes, I only had one course with him, but I had some conversations with him after class, and when I was writing my dissertation, and they made a strong impression on me."

"What was the most important lesson you learned from him?"

She smiled. "Mr. MacIver always insisted that, whatever I was learning about historical methods in the course of my degree, I should never surrender the conviction (they were his words, I can still hear the Scottish burring of his *r*'s scornfully on the word *surrender*) that a historian must involve himself passionately in the lives of the people he is studying. He has to understand the minute variances that are the real prime movers of historical change: the choices an individual can make, from the identical background as everyone around him, to crave something for himself and his family that is entirely different from the 'popular' choice. He was a notoriously passionate man himself, and I think quite a few of his colleagues disapproved of him or were afraid of him."

"He sounds quite a character. Is he still alive?"

She looked embarrassed for a moment. "I don't know. I remember hearing that his wife had died sometime last year. But I'm ashamed to say I don't know if he's still alive."

"Me neither, Katherine," said MacIver to himself as he switched off the program and shuffled off to bed. But he was very grateful to her. As he lay on the bed under the navy greatcoat waiting for sleep, if it ever came, he thought: "You've been wrong so many times, but you can't have been wrong every time."

Release

It turned out Katherine Corton was visiting friends in Well-fleet two days later, and decided to inquire about Robert MacIver; her embarrassment in the interview proceeded from her sense that she had been negligent towards her old mentor. She should find out about him. She was a good researcher, and decided to start at the hub, the local supermarket, and particularly with Bonnie, the checkout clerk.

"Do you know Robert MacIver?"

"The old Scottish professor? Sure."

"Do you know if he's still alive?

"Oh, good heavens, yes, he must be. He's a good, gruff friend to us all here, and we would have heard if he'd died. But come to think of it, I haven't seen him for months. He did a huge load of shopping well before Christmas—October, even September—and that's the last time I saw him."

"Do you think he could have gone to Florida, or somewhere?"

"I really doubt it. One winter in filthy weather I said to him, 'Will you be going south, Mr. MacIver?' and he said, 'Never, Bonnie, never. Scotsmen should never be cooked in the sun.' But this is really worrying." She asked around the store, and no one had seen him.

Bonnie was persistent, and phoned her boyfriend, Matt, a fireman. Matt said that in his rounds snow-clearing, he had noticed Mr. MacIver's driveway was not plowed. He had assumed he was away. He would come with his pickup in an hour, and they would go and check on him. Would Katherine care to come with them? Katherine introduced herself, and said she would.

Matt turned up promptly with his big Dodge truck, with plow attached, and they climbed up next to him. They went down the back roads, through the woods, and found the remote MacIver driveway blocked with a mountain of icy and gritty snow cast aside by town plows from the road. Matt went to work, bulling the truck in and out, left and right. Once past the first barrier, it was easier through the trees and up to the house. They saw a car mounded in snow, and they saw the porch of the house collapsed. Matt gave three loud blares on the horn.

"This could be grisly," he said in warning. "But we should go in."

MacIver meanwhile was still there, but barely. He had fallen out of his rocking chair, and was now lying, slightly dazed, on his side, with one hand under his head—reclining, really. Suddenly, he thought, the door opened. There were people there, and it seemed light and cold had come in with them. They were still over by the door, uncertain what they had found. He summoned the last ounce of graciousness he had left to greet them: "Hello," he said. "I think I may need some help." His words released them, and they rushed towards him. But he had been quite quick in his day, and slipped away before they reached him.

Acknowledgments

For a quick man, MacIver has taken a long time coming to light, and many have urged him forward over the years and should now be recognized.

I want to thank Amherst College, and in particular two successive deans, Lisa Raskin and Gregory Call, who have been generous to me with research grants and computer assistance; the Imperial War Museum in London and its library staff, who supplied me in short order with essential information on World War I gas production and casualties; and Columbia University, and especially Professor W. Theodore de Bary, for admission to its genial Society of Senior Scholars.

Two close friends have given me expert advice—Paul Raymond-Barker, a great rugby player, and a soldier and forester besides, and Captain E.H.M. Orme, RN, who provided details of naval gunnery and procedures. And many other friends have read all or part of the book and commented on it knowingly. The most long-suffering of these should be named: Michael Rosenthal and Daniel Dolgin heard so many MacIver stories at so many lunches that by the end they both indicated a defensive preference for making up their own. But MacIver believed that old friends should be *tested*. I want to thank them here, and a host of others who gave focused comments and help at key times; you start to write a first novel with doubt, but I became conscious of a resonant chorus in the air around me, strong with the insistence that the time comes when you stop talking and finish what you have begun.

The oldest story is that a book goes nowhere unless it is adopted or espoused, and then advanced, and here I have been preternaturally lucky. My friend Elisabeth Gitter read the manuscript and showed it to Molly Friedrich, who cannily sent it to Ileene Smith to read and edit, who in turn urged Alison Samuel to allow it entry into England: never in this game was a man so blessed with such a stylish quadruple play.

Unless it was in his family. My children, Chris, Maggie, and Emily, and their sweet consorts, Victoria and Matt, have recognized, I fear, pale facets of their lively selves in some of these pages but have still generously accepted the story and encouraged me. But the whole thing must be for Katherine, because, even through its faintest days, she kept willing it into life.

www.randomhouse.co.uk/vintage